Time for Love

Wild Rose Ridge
Book 4

Kathy Geary Anderson

© 2023 by Kathy Geary Anderson

All rights reserved. No part of this book may be reproduced or used in any manner without written permission of the copyright owner except for the use of quotations in a book review.

This is a work of fiction. Where real people, events, establishments, organizations, or locales appear, they are used fictitiously. All other elements of the novel are drawn from the author's imagination.

Edited by Kristin Avila

Cover by EDH Professionals

ISBN 978-1-7369207-6-3 (paperback)

Published by Purple Autumn Press

www.kathygearyanderson.com

❀ Created with Vellum

Acknowledgments

As always, the production of a book does not take place in a vacuum. My thanks go out to all the following:

To my husband, Kurt, for putting up with all the times I'm off living in my imaginary worlds.

To my editor, Kristin Avila, you continually make my stories stronger.

To Amy Petrowich for your eagle proofreading eye.

To Erin Dameron-Hill of EDH Professionals, thanks for the beautiful cover design.

To my MBT Huddle group—Pattie, Linda, Dalyn, Mary, and Kit—your daily prayers and encouragement are priceless. Thanks for inviting me on this multi-author adventure!

To the Scribe Tribe—Dalyn, Elizabeth, Kim, Jennifer, and Sara–thanks for all your gentle input and support for this writing journey we're on.

To my family and friends who encourage and cheer me along, I value each and every one of you.

To my readers, thank you for taking the time to read my stories. I am honored.

Chapter One

Fiona Jones was all about taking risks, but she may have gone too far this time. Balancing her toes on a two-inch-wide rocky ledge, she stretched toward the crevice in the rock above her. If she could just get a little higher, she could take a picture. A foot or two was all it would take. She searched the rock face for a foothold that would get her that much higher. Everything was smooth. Except. Yes. Maybe that root. Testing it to see if it would hold her weight, she pulled herself higher by grasping a branch of the cedar that hung just above her head. There. She steadied herself against the face of the rock.

In another week or two, pink blossoms would be blooming all over this ridge. It's what Wild Rose Ridge was famous for. Where the town got its name. Why the first blooms of the season had to be perched halfway up a rocky outcropping almost impossible to reach was beyond her. She felt for these valiant little blooms, though. She did. She knew well the struggles of growing where you didn't belong.

Still, they could have made things easier for her by growing a few feet lower on this ridge. Nevertheless, the last two weeks of haunting these hiking paths every day had finally paid off. All she needed was a picture for proof.

Holding tight to the branch with her left hand, she angled her phone above the flowers. The shutter button was almost impossible to reach with her phone turned that way. If she could only . . . there. She heard the satisfying click. A quick check of her screen showed a blurry, off-centered cluster of pink blossoms with bright yellow centers. Not her best shot by far, but it would suffice. Blurry or not, it was all the proof she needed that the first wild roses were finally blooming. Final preparation could begin for the town's annual Wild Rose Days.

At last!

With a few quick swipes, she pulled up the town's social media pages and added the picture to both Facebook and Instagram. The rest could wait until she was back on solid ground.

Fiona slipped her phone into the side pocket of her leggings and started inching down the incline. She'd send a group text to the drama club first. Once the mayor made it official and appointed her as director of the festival play, they'd need to start their final practices right away. Most of the cast knew their lines already. They'd been practicing once a week since January. All those hours she and Adele Langley had spent revamping the original festival play, which was an outdated rendition of the town's history, were finally coming to fruition.

This version of the play was much better than the previous one. Not only had they given the Indian princess a name—Tehya—they'd fleshed out the love triangle between her, Jakob Jeremiah Kohlmann, and Gertrude Schulte. And they'd taken out that awful double suicide that had been the ending to the original play. The Schultes and Colemans in town should be happy about that.

A rock beneath her left foot slipped, snapping her attention back to her descent. Fiona threw all her weight to the right but couldn't keep her balance. Pain ratcheted through her leg as her hip cracked against something sharp. The next few seconds passed in a blur as she slid and rolled across the rocky surface of the slope and landed with a thud on the path below. Crud. That hurt!

She lay still for a minute, testing her injuries. Luckily, she'd been halfway down before she slipped. She'd only fallen, well, actually slid, four or five feet. Still, her entire right leg was pounding from hip to knee. Her cheek stung, and her backside ached from where she'd landed on it.

Worst of all, she'd torn her favorite pair of leggings. Blood oozed from a gash that ran mid-thigh to her knee. Dizziness waved through her. She'd never liked blood. Especially her own blood. And that gash looked deep. She blew out a breath. She couldn't faint. Not here. Not now.

Gritting her teeth, she pushed to her feet. Ow. This wasn't going to be easy. But she could do it. All she needed was to make it back to her car. She'd deal with cleaning up that cut when she got to her apartment. She didn't have time to be hurt. She had a full day ahead of her. Now that the first wild rose had been spotted, the mayor might call a town meeting as early as tonight. In fact, . . . she pulled her phone out of her pocket to make a quick check for any responses to the picture she'd posted.

Oh no. No. No. No.

A million cracks spider-webbed across the screen. When her hip hit that first big rock, her phone must have taken a beating too. She touched the fingerprint sensor to turn the phone on and ran her finger tentatively across the screen. Thankfully, the screen protector kept the glass shards from splintering and falling out. But the screen wasn't right. Half of it was off-centered, and nothing moved when she tried scrolling through the icons.

She tapped her text message icon. Nothing. Then, the phone icon. Still nothing. This was not good. She couldn't even call Benedict to tell him to open the bookstore for her. She doubted she'd be able to hobble off this mountain in time to do it herself, and this leg would need some attention. She glanced down at the gash to see blood trickling down her leg and pooling in her sock. Queasiness overwhelmed. She hobbled to the nearest boulder and sat, head down between her knees. *Don't faint. Breathe.*

Dear God, what am I supposed to do?

Keeping her eyes firmly fixed on the pebbled path beneath her, she drew in another breath and slowly let it out. She could do this if she kept her eyes off that awful gash. Once her head cleared, she'd head toward her car. Maybe she'd meet another hiker on her way down. But what were the chances of that? Not many got up at the crack of dawn to hike this trail, especially this early in the season. In the past week, she'd encountered no more than two other hikers on her daily excursions, but maybe . . . *Lord, please? A little help would be appreciated.*

One more deep breath, then she slowly raised herself to a sitting position and stood. It was fine. She was fine. She could do this with or without help. She'd certainly had enough practice doing things for herself over the years. Today would be no different.

This bike ride was exactly what he needed. Chase Coleman careened down the steep path. He hadn't been on a mountain bike in years, but his cousin, Jason, was right. He couldn't let his old motorcycle accident keep him from doing all the other things he loved. He was an avid cyclist long before he ever climbed on Arlan's Roadmaster.

Taking this particular road up the ridge might have been pushing things a bit, but Jason's mountain bike felt a lot more comfortable than Arlan's motorcycle ever did. Chase's bike skills came back to him right away. Sure, he'd taken the curves a lot slower than he would have in the past, but he hadn't felt any of the anxiety he had expected. Maybe time had healed that wound more than he would have thought.

He was glad now that he had listened to Jason when

he'd offered him the use of his bike. He couldn't keep up the work pace of the last two weeks without some sort of daily exercise. He'd dig his own bike out of storage and find a way to work this into his schedule somehow.

Today he had plenty of time—his first day off since he came home two weeks ago. But what a two weeks it had been. He'd thought working the emergency room of a Seattle hospital was stressful. Apparently, becoming a partner in a small-town doctor's office could be just as crazy. Especially if anyone and everyone in town decided to make an appointment to see what the hometown boy was like as a doctor. Doc Johnson said things would slow down soon. Chase sure hoped so.

In the meantime, he planned to enjoy this day off. A bike ride to start it, and then he would help Dad at the vineyard. Part of the reason he'd moved back was to be available at Rose Cove. He'd been shocked at how old and tired his dad looked on his last visit three months ago. Little had changed since then. The man was trying to do too much.

Once things settled a little at the practice, Chase would convince Dad to come in for a full workup. See if anything besides stress was causing him to be so tired. Aunt Violet had told him she didn't think Rose Cove Vineyards was doing so well. So far, Dad had made no mention of it, but then, they hadn't found much time to talk. But he'd only just moved back. He'd make the time. Today, for a start.

Chase couldn't believe he was thinking this, but he almost wished Oliver would come back. His brother knew the business side of things much better than Chase did. But Oliver was busy chasing his dream of being a Los Angeles real estate magnate. He doubted he'd ever be satisfied with the slow-paced life of Wild Rose Ridge. It was exactly the life Chase wanted, however.

Slowing on the next corner, he braked and hopped off his bike, walking to the edge of a sharp drop-off. This. This was why he'd come home. He'd always loved the view from this overlook. He breathed in the fresh scent of the crisp mountain morning. In front of him, Wild Rose Lake stretched into the distance, the sun glinting off the water in ever-moving sparkles. Had the water always been that blue?

He'd missed this. The mornings. The beauty. His family. Yep. It was good to be home. And just because Oliver was the businessman of the family didn't mean Chase couldn't help Dad. He'd grown up pruning vines and spraying rows with the rest of them. Dad and Grandpa Ben had seen to that. None of the three Coleman children had been exempt from work in the vineyards.

Chase mounted his bike again. Time to get back. He'd promised Dad he'd help mow between the vines later this morning. He was looking forward to it, in fact. He needed the outdoor work almost as much as he'd needed this ride. Much as he loved being a doctor, he was definitely ready for a break.

He spun around another bend, then slowed when he spotted a girl hobbling down the path ahead. Blisters? Or maybe a turned ankle. Hiking this rocky terrain could be brutal if you weren't used to it. Drawing closer, he spotted a bloody gash staining the girl's right leg.

"Need help?"

She jumped and whirled around, her long, red braid swinging as she turned. Blue eyes, almost black with pain, stared up at him. Wow. She was a stunner.

"Looks like you're hurt."

Her eyes became guarded. "I'm fine. I'll be fine. I just need to get to my car."

"The parking lot is still a mile and a half from here. And that gash on your leg looks pretty nasty. Mind if I look at it? I'm a doctor. I can help." He didn't blame her for her skeptical look. It wasn't like he always carried a medical kit with him. And other than looking at the injury, there wasn't much he could do to help until he could get her to the first aid kit in his truck.

"I'm sure it's fine." She glanced down at her leg, then paled.

He hopped off the bike and took hold of her arm. "Whoa. Better sit down before you faint." He led her to a nearby boulder and helped her sit.

"It's the blood. I'm not so good with it."

He nodded. "Lots of people aren't. Try looking at that tree over there while I look at the gash. No need for both of us to look at it." He examined the cut. Deep. It was going to need stitches for sure. And plenty of cleaning to remove all the dirt and gravel embedded in it. Luckily no veins or arteries had been cut. Blood still oozed from the wound, but there was no danger of too much blood loss. "How'd it happen?"

"I missed a step and slipped down that ridge back there. I must have scraped my leg across a sharp rock when I was falling."

"Are you hurt anywhere else?"

She held up her left arm to show him a scrape from her elbow to her wrist. He could see another similar scrape on her cheek—road rash mostly, in both places.

"Did you hit your head at all?" He looked into her eyes, checking her pupils. No dilation.

"Maybe," she said. "But not hard. It all happened so fast. My leg hurts the most."

He grabbed an unopened water bottle from his backpack.

"This might sting a bit." He slowly poured water on the gash, dislodging some of the dirt and small pebbles that coated the wound. He wouldn't be able to get all the dirt until he got her back to the clinic, where he could flush it out properly. Taking a clean t-shirt from his backpack, he wrapped it around her leg, tying the ends to hold it. "That'll do until we get you back to the parking lot. It's going to need stitches. And deep cleaning. The sooner we get to it, the better."

"Stitches? Are you sure?"

"Positive. But getting you off this mountain is our first challenge." He looked over at Jason's bike and then back at her. With her slim frame, she couldn't weigh more than 120 pounds. He knew better than to ask, of course. He pushed to his feet. "Come on. I'll give you a ride."

"On what? Your bike? No way. I'd rather walk. One fall is plenty for one day."

"Trust me. I've given my sister rides lots of times." Granted, they had both been kids at the time, and those rides hadn't been on a rocky mountain path. He was sure he could do it, though, or he wouldn't have suggested it.

"It's either ride with me on the bike and be down in five minutes or continue to hobble along and take thirty. Look, this bike even has a tandem seat." He pointed to the small kid's seat attached to the front bar. Thank goodness he hadn't taken the time to take it off earlier. "My cousin's kids ride on it all the time."

"It's a kid's seat. It's not going to hold me. And there's no way my feet will fit in those stirrups. They're way too short."

"Look." He rolled the bike parallel to the boulder she was sitting on. "All you need to do is stand on the boulder and lower yourself onto the seat sideways. If you put most of your weight on your left side, it shouldn't hurt the cut on your leg. Try it."

By the look on her face, he wasn't going to win any confidence awards any time soon, but she stood up, stepped onto the rock, and eyed the seat.

"You're sure I'll fit on that?"

"You'll absolutely fit. Trust me."

"Shouldn't I straddle it?"

"You could, but you'd have to hold your legs straight out in front of you, or they'll get in the way of my peddling. I think it'll be easier if you sit sideways. Let your legs dangle off the side."

He held the bike steady while she tried it. As he suspected, she fit on the seat just fine. She was a tiny little thing, not much bigger than a child herself. She winced as she settled into position.

"You okay?"

"Yeah. It's not bad."

"Good. I'm going to get on behind you now. I'll need

to start peddling right away to keep the bike balanced. Hold onto the handlebars in the middle and try not to move around too much."

He pushed off as he mounted the bike, and they were on their way. The trick would be to keep the bike from picking up too much speed on the way down. With the extra weight, things could easily get unbalanced.

Because she needed to lean back against him to keep the weight off her hurt leg, it felt as if she was wrapped in his arms. The position should have felt awkward since they were practically strangers, but somehow it didn't. It felt nice. Too nice. He could smell the slightly floral scent of her shampoo as strands of her hair brushed against his face. If he didn't know better, he would think she almost snuggled into him on that last curve. Most likely, she was merely trying to keep her balance.

Five minutes later, they reached the parking lot at the trailhead. Only two cars were parked there. His truck and what he assumed was her Subaru.

"It might be best if I give you a ride to the clinic. We can come back and pick up your car later. I'd like to get that cut cleaned out and stitched right away."

She heaved a soft sigh. "Fine. But could I use your phone first? Mine got crushed when I fell, and I need to call my assistant to open my shop."

She punched a number into his phone and waited. Frustration edged her mouth when the person on the other end failed to pick up. She blew out a breath and punched in another number.

"Ivy. Hey. It's me. Yeah. I know. I borrowed his phone. Look, I've had a fall and will need some stitches.

No. No. It's fine. It's nothing major. I promise. But I can't open the shop right now, and Benedict won't pick up. He's supposed to be in by ten, but the Mama and Me Tea Party starts at nine. Any chance you could . . . you will? Thanks, girl. I owe you. Yeah, the scones you made are in the back fridge. I'll fill you in later. I promise. I *will*. Bye!"

"You know my cousin, Ivy?"

"Best friends."

"So, you know who I—"

"Everyone knows who you are, Dr. Coleman. It's not every day the town welcomes a new doctor."

"You better call me Chase, then. Dr. Coleman is way too stuffy for a friend of my cousin. I guess I never asked you for your name either."

"I'm Fiona. Fiona Jones."

Fiona. Why did that name sound so familiar? He knew a lot of Ivy's friends but didn't remember any this gorgeous. If they'd met before, he would have remembered.

"Nice to meet you, Fiona. Too bad it couldn't be under better circumstances. Now. Let's get you to the clinic to get you stitched up."

Chapter Two

He didn't remember her. Not that she'd expected him to remember a scrawny thirteen-year-old he'd not seen for almost fourteen years. Still. Now that he knew she was Ivy's best friend, shouldn't that have jogged his memory . . . a little? Or when he'd heard her name, at least? How many Fionas had he known over the years? She'd be willing to bet she was the only one. The name wasn't that common.

She'd known way back then that her childhood crush on Chase Coleman had been entirely one-sided. After all, she'd been a lowly middle schooler while he'd been heading into his junior year of high school. He'd known who she was, though. He'd known her well enough to tease and pick on her whenever she and Ivy were around. He'd call her "Princess" with an awful Irish accent and ask her if she'd seen Shrek. And yet, today, she told him her name, and he didn't even remember her.

All of that wouldn't have mattered if he'd somehow turned out to be ugly or out-of-shape. Or if he'd become a full-of-himself, know-it-all like some brilliant, young doctors. Instead, he was ripped, handsome, and still sporting that little boy smile that made all the girls melt. And he was kind and friendly and even a bit funny. No. Chase Coleman had only gotten better with age.

And he didn't remember her at all.

Thirteen-year-old Fiona would have thought she'd died and gone to heaven during that bike ride down the mountain. The thought of having Chase Coleman's arms around her for any reason back then would have sent her into a swoon. Twenty-six-year-old Fiona was more concerned with keeping her hurt leg from bouncing too much and not falling off the bike. That didn't mean she hadn't appreciated his strong biceps and proximity. She'd noticed. A lot. It had taken all her willpower not to snuggle into his chest on the ride down. Thankfully, the ride was short.

"Here we are." Chase pulled his pickup into the back lot of the Wild Rose Ridge clinic. "Sit tight a minute, and I'll come around and help you climb out."

She would have liked to have made it out of the truck on her own terms, but she was glad for Chase's help since her leg had stiffened up on their drive into town. Trying to bend it sent a shot of fire from her knee to her hip.

"I'll take you in the back, so you won't have to traipse through the waiting room." Chase glanced at his watch. "The clinic doesn't officially open for another fifteen minutes, but there may be patients out front already. Since this is my day off, there's no need to complicate things." He opened the office's back door, then led her down a hallway to a small exam room. "Hop up on the table while I go get my supplies. It's important that we get that cut thoroughly cleaned before we stitch it. That's why I wanted to bring you here to do it. Our nurse, Lydia, is an expert at that kind of thing."

Left alone, Fiona stared at the photograph of Wild Rose Lake that hung on the wall across from her. Anything to keep her mind off the cut and the upcoming procedure. She didn't like blood, but she really, really didn't like pain. She was glad Chase had wrapped her leg back on the trail, so there was little chance of her looking at the cut. She assumed the t-shirt he'd wrapped around it had stopped the bleeding, but she wasn't willing to look at it to find out. She didn't need to add fainting to her list of things that had gone wrong this morning.

She hoped Ivy was okay handling the Mama and Me Tea Party. Not that her friend wouldn't be. Ivy was perfect for that sort of thing. Her scones and berry tarts were always the hit of the party. But mornings were the busiest times at Ivy's mom's bakery. Especially Saturday mornings. She hated pulling Ivy away from that, but it couldn't be helped. Benedict certainly wasn't the man for the job. He was a great help in the bookstore, but kids were not his forte—especially excited little girls in twirly dresses and hats.

Chase came back in, followed close behind by Lydia Lighthorse.

"This is our nurse extraordinaire, Lydia."

"I know." Fiona smiled at the forty-something woman in blue scrubs who played the part of Tehya's mother in the festival play. "No t-ball this morning?"

"One game this morning and two this afternoon.

Mike's handling the chauffeur duties today since this is my weekend to work. Chase tells me you fell on your hike this morning. Would that be before or after you posted the wild rose picture?"

"After. My phone's worse off from the fall than I am."

"Bummer. Word's spreading, though. Gianna texted the drama club. And it sounds like the mayor has scheduled the town meeting for Monday night."

Monday night. Good. Tonight would have been better, but she supposed that would have been too quick a turnaround, even for a small town.

Chase cleared his throat. "Should we tackle this leg now?"

"Oh. Of course, doctor. I'm sorry."

As Lydia unwrapped Chase's t-shirt from around her leg, Fiona focused once again on the lake photograph. A pretty spot. A black and white picture of rows of vines sloping down toward the lake that shimmered in the sunlight. Could it have been taken from Rose Cove Vineyards? Maybe Tori had taken it. Chase's sister was an award-winning photojournalist who traveled the world. Ivy said she was working somewhere in France these days.

"Fiona. Did you hear me?" Lydia's voice broke through her wanderings.

"Hmmm?"

"I'm sorry, hon. We're going to have to cut your leggings."

Her favorite leggings? Crud. She'd paid way too much for those, but they were torn beyond repair anyway.

Once all the buttery soft fabric was cut away, Chase and Lydia got down to business.

"You might want to lay down for this," Chase said.

Good idea. She'd seen the blood oozing from the cut again and was already feeling woozy.

"I irrigated the wound with water before I wrapped it, but it needs to be thoroughly flushed," Chase told Lydia.

Lydia nodded and went to the nearby cabinet. She returned with a large syringe and a basin.

Fiona winced as the solution stung the wound. Deep breaths. She wasn't about to lose it in front of Chase. She closed her eyes and concentrated on breathing like Genevieve Peters had taught them in yoga class.

"That should do it," Chase said after Lydia had worked on her leg for a minute or two or ten. "Let's go ahead and numb it. I'll look at it more carefully after the anesthetic takes effect. You'll feel a little bit of a sting here, Fiona, but then things should get better."

Ow. A little sting? Why did doctors always say a "little" sting when what they truly meant was pure fire? Fiona forced out the breath she was holding and imagined Genevieve's gentle, "Breathe in, two, three, four, now release, two, three, four. And again."

"Are you feeling that now? Fiona?"

"What? No. Just a little pressure is all."

"Good. Hold tight. This may take a bit. Your gash is pretty long. You must have ripped across something sharp on your way down that incline. Probably a rock. Looks like you're going to have a pretty big bruise on your hip. Was the picture worth it?"

Was it? She probably could have waited a week and

found a rose bush on more level ground, but it was already mid-May. She'd been waiting all winter to debut her new script at the Wild Rose Days festival. Waiting another week had seemed impossible earlier this morning. But now, with what was sure to be a scar clear down her leg and the loss of her favorite leggings, she wasn't so sure.

"Maybe not. But what's done is done."

The room grew silent except for Chase humming a little under his breath. Was that "Love Story"? Somehow, she hadn't pictured Chase as a Swiftie. She didn't know him well enough to tease him about it, but honestly, there was something very endearing about him singing something so sweet while working on something so gory. At least he enjoyed his work. She couldn't imagine anyone looking at exposed, raw flesh and enjoying it. Just the thought sent her back to her deep breathing exercises.

"All done now." Chase squeezed her calf, sending a tingle of awareness straight through her body. Should she be embarrassed that her childhood crush had seen so much of her bare skin today? Not that any of that mattered. It wasn't like he even remembered who she was. Clearly, she had meant very little to him back then.

He helped her sit up. "We should probably clean up the rest of you now. I see Lydia has everything ready for us. Thank you. Also, Fiona, do you remember when you had your last tetanus shot by any chance?"

Tetanus? Shoot. Mom was always great at getting her all her shots growing up, especially each time they left the country. But since she'd come back to the states for college, she'd let all that slip.

"I'm not sure. It could be ten years or more."

He glanced at his watch. "I'll finish up here if you could get a shot ready for me, Lydia. Then I'll let you get back to today's patients."

"No worries. Saturdays are usually slow. Unless our new doctor is on duty. Let's hope the town doesn't take note of your pickup in the back lot. We could get really busy, really quick." She shot Fiona a smile as she exited the room.

As Chase took her left arm and began gently cleaning it, Fiona could see why the patients flocked to see him. He was a good doctor. Friendly, caring, thorough. And too darn handsome for his own good. But she wasn't going down that road again. She learned her lesson in middle school. Giving her whole heart to someone who didn't even care if she existed was something she'd never do again.

He finished bandaging her arm and then turned his attention to her face. Cupping her chin with his fingers, he turned her head up and to the side. His index finger grazed her cheek, feather-light yet sending a tremor through her. He stood so close she could smell his aftershave. The scent brought back their ride down the mountain and the feel of his strong arms wrapped around her. She took a deep breath and pulled back.

"Sorry. I didn't mean to hurt you. That one's not deep, but I should clean it. You don't want to flirt with an infection."

No, but she wouldn't mind flirting with him.

Stop it. She wasn't going there again. She closed her eyes to shut out his proximity and tried to think of something else. Anything else other than the man standing oh so close. He made quick work of the ointment and dressing, then tapped her gently on the other cheek.

"All done, Princess."

Her eyes flew open. Had he said what she thought he'd said? And with that awful Irish accent?

His grin said it all. The same grin that had melted her thirteen-year-old heart a million times over.

"What? You thought I'd forgotten you, Princess Fiona? It took me a while, but I finally remembered why your name seemed so familiar. You are Ivy's pen-pal friend, right? The one who lived in Africa somewhere?"

She nodded. "Kenya, mostly. Early years in Uganda."

"Your parents are missionaries, right?"

"Yes. They started out digging wells for villages all over Uganda. They've branched out into Kenya, Tanzania, and Sudan now."

"That must have been quite a childhood. Growing up in all those places. What brought you to Wild Rose Ridge?"

The stability, for one. Wild Rose Ridge was the only place she remembered feeling remotely like home. The first place she ever remembered having a best friend. But Chase didn't need to hear all that.

She shrugged. "My grandparents left me their lake house right about the time I finished college. It seemed like as good a place as any to settle down. Plus, Ivy was here. We'd roomed together in college for a few years. She had come back here after culinary school. I decided to come too. I opened a tea and bookstore on Main and haven't looked back yet."

"You have a store? That's great. I'll have to stop by sometime." He glanced at the clock on the wall. "But I'm guessing you'd like to get on with your day. I can drop you by your shop if you'd like, but you better hold off driving for a while since the stitches are in your right leg. Do you need help getting your car home?"

"No. I'll be fine. Ivy and Benedict can help me later. And don't worry about getting me home. I had Lydia call Ivy for me, and she's on her way. You've done enough for me already."

"I don't mind." The look in those dark chocolate eyes of his almost had her believing him. Which was another reason she would let Ivy help her, not him. Some trouble wasn't worth chasing.

Chase found Dad checking the Syrahs on the far end of the property. He looked tired. Too tired. They hadn't had any opportunity to talk one-on-one since Chase had come home. The clinic had kept him hopping since day one. And then today, Fiona's accident had taken all his morning. Not that he was sorry.

Well, of course, he was sorry she'd been hurt. He wasn't sorry to have run into her, though. She'd been a funny little thing as a kid. Dramatic. Full of stories and passion. Now she was all grown up and gorgeous. He was looking forward to knowing her as an adult.

Dad turned from the vine he'd been examining.

"'Bout time you showed up. What happened to

helping with the mowing this morning?" Dad's grin told him he wasn't serious.

"Sorry about that. You got my text, right?"

"Yeah. How's your patient?"

"Nothing a few stitches and a little time won't heal. How are the vines looking?"

"So far, so good. No frost since bud break, so we should be ready for shoot thinning in a few more weeks. Think you can help with that?"

"I'll do my best. Doc Johnson has promised me every other weekend off, plus Tuesday and Thursday mornings. Evenings too, if needed. What's your crew look like?"

"It's been tough finding workers. Pete Sandina and his family, of course. And we hired a couple of summer interns from WSU, but they won't start until the end of May." Dad heaved a big breath.

"You look tired, Dad. Sure you're feeling okay? When was the last time you had a full physical? Might not be a bad idea to schedule one."

"I'm fine. You know as well as I do that we fruit farmers don't get much sleep in the spring. In another week or two, when all danger of frost is over, I'll get rested again."

They had reached the top of the row, and both turned to look out on the vines stretched in long rows down the ridge toward Wild Rose Lake. The view from Rose Cove Vineyards was second to none. He hadn't realized how good he'd had it growing up until he'd left home.

"How are the new Syrahs and Rieslings coming

along? Have you found any potential buyers yet? Other than High Ridge, of course. With all the new wineries in the area, I'd think some would be interested in supplementing their supply."

"A few. A new winery on the North shore reached out to me last week. I think we'll be able to make a deal. I've dropped all our contracts with High Ridge. I'm not going to work with an outfit I can't trust."

Dad shot a glare toward the vines to the north of them. High Ridge had been a thorn in their family business for years. What had once been a neighborly partnership turned sour five years back when the Morales family refused at the last minute to buy the grapes they'd contracted, saying they didn't meet their standards. Most of that year's harvest had gone to waste since the other wineries in the area already had the grapes they needed. Dad and Grandpa had managed to sell some at a greatly reduced price to a small jelly company that sold wine jellies and jams, but the vineyard had yet to make up for that loss. The monetary loss was one thing, but the hit to their reputation as quality grape growers hurt the worst.

"Everything they have came from our family. Those vines over there?" Dad pointed to the prize Lembergers on the neighboring section of land. "Those were ours. Our ancestors brought the parent vines to this country. So how did High Ridge end up with them? Tell me that."

Chase shrugged. He'd heard the story before, first from Grandpa. Now, Dad. Yet no one seemed to know how the Morales family ended up with the grapes that supposedly belonged to the Coleman ancestors.

"They stole our vines. Now they want to steal the

whole vineyard. Did I tell you they offered to buy us out again? At a third of what the land is worth. Their land is no better than ours. We have the same soil and the same exposure to the sun. And yet, the wines from their grapes somehow win rave reviews while ours are considered substandard? My dad should have never agreed to give them exclusive access to our grapes back when they started their winery. It's like giving a thief the key to all your treasure. They ruin our reputation and now expect to buy our land for a song? I'll be dead and in the grave before I let that happen."

That's exactly what Chase was afraid would happen. This vineyard was stealing Dad's health. A man in his late fifties should not look this old and this tired.

"How's the winemaking coming along?"

Rose Cove had a long way to go before they'd ever catch up with the operation High Ridge Cellars had going. Grandpa Ben had wanted no part in alcohol production of any kind. It was a struggle in the early days to get him to sell his grapes to any winery at all instead of solely to the jelly companies. If René Bouchard hadn't been such a good friend of his and the prices they could get from apple production so low, Grandpa would never have considered it.

Dad hadn't shared his father's distaste for winemaking. Shortly after Grandpa Ben died, Dad decided to add a winery to their vineyard like many neighbors here in Wild Rose Ridge had. He invested a lot of money in new buildings and equipment and threw himself into becoming a vintner.

Dad walked along the row, bending to look at each

branch. "It's slow. I love the process but making a name in the industry takes time. And handling both the vineyard and the winery, well, it's a lot. What we need is for your brother to come home. He'd know how to make a go of it. He's been a success at everything he's ever tried."

Ah. There it was—the age-old mantra. *Oliver can do it. Oliver is the man for the job. Let Oliver handle it, Chase. It's too much for you.* When was Dad going to realize that he was a grown man too? He was perfectly capable of helping the family business. And he *would* help. Oliver had no interest in Rose Cove Vineyards. In fact, if he were to come home, his first order of business would be to find a buyer who would give them the highest price possible. That's what Oliver did. He sold things. He didn't hold onto them and make them better.

But Chase was here now. And busy as the clinic had been this past month, things were sure to slow down. This was Wild Rose Ridge, not Seattle. And when they did, Chase would do everything he could to see that his family's business survived. Five generations on the same soil meant something. Whatever it took, he would not be the generation that let that slip away.

Chapter Three

Rosehip Tea and Books. Even the sign gave a Fiona vibe. Classic with a touch of whimsy. Was a two-day gap long enough not to look desperate in seeking her out again? Normally, Chase would make his own black coffee or grab a quick Americano from Magic Beans on his way to the clinic. Today, he didn't have appointments scheduled until ten, so he was allowing himself the guilty pleasure of checking out Fiona's place. Not that he'd drunk a cup of tea a day in his life. But there was a first time for everything, right? Who knew? Maybe he'd become a pinky-waving connoisseur.

The bell on the heavy door jangled as he opened it and stepped into a shop that smelled of old books and flowers. Small tables and cozy chairs were scattered throughout a room that looked like one big library. Books filled shelves, floor to ceiling, along the walls. Shorter bookshelves were positioned next to chairs and sofas scattered throughout the store. Halfway down the room, a tall, lanky man sat behind a small counter with a cash register, his head buried in a book. A girl tapped furiously on her computer at one of the tables, and a couple of women talked over teacups at a table near the door. Soft jazz played on the speakers.

Cozy and welcoming. He could see why the townspeople liked it here.

Threading between the tables and deeper into the store, he finally spotted her. Fiona. She had her back to him, but he couldn't miss her bright red hair that hung loose today across her shoulders and down her back. Its vibrant color drew him like a moth to a flame. He made his way toward her. She was standing behind a bar, studying the tea menu on a large chalkboard that covered the far wall, a piece of chalk in hand.

"Adding something new?" he asked.

She whirled around, surprise on her face.

"Shouldn't you be administering pills and medical advice by now?"

"Doc Johnson is handling the early appointments today. I'll take the late ones. I thought I'd drop by and see how your leg was doing this morning."

"You mean doctors still make house calls?"

"This one does, apparently."

She tucked a strand of hair behind her ear and smiled. He was glad he stopped by. He'd drink any amount of vile liquid to see the sparkle in those blue eyes. Be the recipient of that smile.

"The leg is fine, doctor. And the arm."

"Cheek too, I see." He barely stopped himself from touching the small scrape still visible on her smooth skin. His finger tingled in memory of her skin's silky feel last

Saturday. He didn't have a valid reason to touch her now. That didn't keep him from craving it, though.

"Can I get you a drink?" She asked.

"I don't suppose you serve coffee here."

"Magic Beans, two doors down, specializes in coffee. You can always get yourself a cup there and come back and browse the books. Otherwise, no. This is a tea shop only."

He could tell she had made that particular speech many times. Well, no help for it. He was going to have to try the stuff.

He scanned the chalkboard behind her but couldn't make heads or tails of it. The Gatsby, The Sherlock, The Scarlet. What kind of flavors were those?

"What do you suggest?" He asked, stalling.

"What type of coffee do you usually drink?"

"Americano. Straight. No sugar."

She studied him with a pursed lip and a slight lift of one of her delicate brows. "Ah. A traditionalist. Maybe the Darcy. That's black tea with a hint of hazelnut. No. I've got it. The Santiago. After *The Old Man and the Sea*. It's a pu-erh tea with a touch of salt and a hint of spice. I've named all the blends after literary characters to go with the bookstore theme." She gestured to the shelves all around her.

"Clever. What's your favorite?"

"I'm partial to the Anne Shirley for obvious reasons." She held up a strand of hair and waved it at him, then narrowed her eyes at his obvious blank look. But, honestly, was he supposed to know this Anne Shirley character?

"You know. *Anne with an E? Anne of Green Gables?*"

No. He didn't know. But wait. "Oh, yeah. I think my sister used to like that book. She carried it around a lot as a kid."

"Anne was a redhead." She looked like she was a little annoyed that she'd had to explain.

"Right. So. Maybe the Santiago?

She took down a glass canister from the shelves behind her and pulled out a tea bag. "I could make it a latte for you, but I'm guessing if you're an Americano, no-sugar-kind-of-guy, you'll want it straight."

"Yeah. Just the tea is fine."

She messed around behind the counter for a minute. Then handed him a cup. "Let that steep for a minute or two before you take the bag out. Then, I'd suggest you leave the lid off for another couple of minutes. That water's boiling hot."

"Got it. How much do I owe you?"

"This one's on the house. Consider it payback for the bike ride down the mountain."

He laughed and sniffed the drink. Why did he have a feeling he was going to enjoy this tea about as much as she'd enjoyed that ride?

Something bumped against his leg. He jumped, spilling some of the hot liquid on his hand. "Ouch!"

"What happened?" Fiona leaned over the counter. "Oh, it's Charlotte."

A large, calico cat curled around his legs, leaving cat hair on his dark pants. Chase set the hot cup of tea on the counter and grabbed a napkin to wipe his hand.

"Don't you like cats?"

He preferred dogs but didn't think he'd win any points admitting that. "Of course, I like cats. I wasn't expecting her was all." He squatted down to rub Charlotte under the chin. She gave him a typical queen cat stare, then turned and walked away, which was exactly why he preferred dogs.

"Don't worry. Charlotte takes a while to warm up to people. I'm surprised she came over to rub against you this soon. She usually only does that to people who don't care for cats. She can sense it somehow."

Great. He'd been outed by a cat.

Fiona handed him his to-go cup, this time without the tea bag and with a lid.

"We wouldn't want any more accidents." Her eyes teased. "Are you going to the town meeting tonight?"

"I didn't know there was one."

"It's for the Wild Rose Days festival. Only two weeks away now that the roses are blooming. The mayor will be setting up all the committees. You should come."

Like he needed something else to add to his schedule. He was almost maxed out between getting started at the clinic and helping Dad at the vineyard. He hadn't been to Wild Rose Days since his senior year in high school when Mrs. Langley made him play Jakob Jeremiah Kohlmann in the annual play. Though he loved acting in school plays, the role of his long-dead ancestor hadn't been his favorite. It had kind of a hokey plot if he remembered correctly. But the festival could be fun and finding some way to redeem himself in Fiona's eyes after the cat and *Anne with an E* missteps could be worth it.

"What time is the meeting?"

"Seven o'clock. At town hall."

"If my appointments don't go too long, I should be able to make it. See you then?"

Her smile was his reward.

"I'll be there."

Two minutes later, he ran into his cousin Arlan on the sidewalk by the lake. Arlan's uncle was married to Chase's aunt, which in Wild Rose Ridge meant he was family. Cousin was the easiest way to categorize it. He, Jason, Arlan, and Oliver had spent a large portion of their family gatherings together, playing ball and getting into all sorts of trouble.

"Hey, Chase." Arlan clapped him on the shoulder. "I heard you were back in town. Good to have you back, man."

"Good to be back. I've missed it."

Arlan eyed the cup in his hand with its prominent Rosehips Tea logo.

"You drink tea now? Times have changed."

"Not really. Just checking on a patient."

Arlan raised a brow. "At the bookstore?"

"Fiona Jones. I had to put some stitches in her on Saturday."

"Ah, yes. The fair Fiona. That girl will go to great lengths to support her town. I was sorry to hear she'd hurt herself getting a picture of the first wild roses."

He shouldn't be surprised that Arlan knew all about Saturday's adventure. News always traveled fast in a small town. It would take some getting used to again, though.

"You coming to the meeting tonight?" Arlan asked.

He supposed, as mayor, Arlan had to recruit everyone he could.

"Seven o'clock, right?"

"That's right. I could use your help on one of the committees."

"I'm not sure I'd have time for that. I'm just starting up at the clinic."

"That's exactly why you should get involved. The people here in the Ridge are all about community. It will go a long way with them to see that their doctor is willing to participate in town events."

Like any politician, Arlan had learned to spin things to his advantage. Chase shrugged. What could it hurt? It was only a two-week commitment. And he'd have an excuse to see Fiona again. Maybe he would volunteer to be on whatever committee she joined.

"If my appointments don't run long, I'll try to be there."

"Good to hear. I'll be looking for you."

Chase waved him on and headed toward the clinic. He took a sip of his now sufficiently cooled tea as he walked. Not terrible. It kind of had a smoky flavor to it. He'd need a good old cup of black coffee as soon as he got to the office, though, or he wouldn't be making it through this day. He was pretty sure Hemingway would agree. From what he knew about the author, he was more likely to sip on a dry martini than a cup of tea. A guy like that probably liked his coffee black.

∽

"Hurry. I want to make sure we get a good seat." Fiona half-jogged along the sidewalk toward the Wild Rose Ridge Community Center. Her best friend, Ivy Weaver, lagged a few steps behind.

"I don't think that'll be a problem. Jeremy said he'd save seats for all the drama club members. He was there half an hour ago setting up. If I'd known we were going to jog to the meeting, I'd have put on my jogging shoes."

"You don't own a pair of jogging shoes."

"My point, exactly. Slow down." Ivy tucked her arm into Fiona's, forcing her to do just that. "The meeting doesn't start for another thirty minutes. We'll get there in plenty of time. Besides, Arlan appointing you as the play committee director is simply a formality. Mrs. Langley gave him your name as her successor six months ago when she left town. Everyone knows you'll be taking her place."

"I know. But I'm looking forward to getting started officially. I can't wait to bring the new version of *Where the Wild Roses Bloom* to the stage. Do you think the town will love it?"

"I know they will. All the cast members do. It's a great improvement over the old play, which was a snooze-inducer, in my opinion. Including Tehya's diary entries and those love letters was a game changer."

"If you hadn't asked your mom to hire me to go through all her great aunt's papers for that estate sale, I never would have found them. I owe you, girl."

They'd reached the steps leading up to WRR's Community Center.

"Fiona. Ivy." A shout from down the street drew their

attention. Katie Rose, who played Gertrude Schulte in the play, waved to them from a block away. "Hold up."

As she caught up to them, she held up her phone. "Jeremy just texted. He has seats saved for all of us on the front left side. He said he roped off a section and put a drama club sign on it."

"Good," Fiona said. "Do you know if all the others are going to make it? We should probably set a time for rehearsal tomorrow. I'm guessing at least three rehearsals this week and every night next week. What do you two think? Mr. Davis said we could use the school auditorium all next week, but they have a couple of end-of-year choir and band concerts we'll have to work around this week. I think we should find an off-site place to rehearse at least part of the time so that we won't fall too far behind. But we can discuss all that once everyone gets here."

She led the way to the left front side of the meeting room, where three rows of folding chairs had been blocked off. Bless Jeremy. The lanky high schooler was a jack-of-all-trades for all the high school drama performances. He was a master of sound, lighting, and set design. He had offered his services for the town's drama club last January. He'd been a godsend already when it came to using the school's sound system. The few practices they'd had so far at the high school had gone so much better with his skills.

Townspeople soon began to trickle into the room. As each drama club member arrived, she waved them toward their section. The room was abuzz with excitement as the various committee members greeted each other. Rose Stevens, who owned the dance studio, and all the dance moms gathered in a group behind theirs. Rose's dancers would perform a ballet rendition of the Wild Rose legend. Fiona had interviewed her about it on the podcast a few weeks ago.

Rose waved and came over.

"I heard about your accident on Saturday. I'm guessing that's what kept you from yoga class this morning?"

In addition to dance classes, Rose's studio offered yoga for all ages. Fiona usually took the early class on Mondays, Wednesdays, and Fridays.

"Yes. I told Genevieve I probably won't be back until the stitches come out."

"Take your time. You don't want to rush it and risk doing more damage."

Ivy's mom waved to them from across the room. Fiona waved back. She loved this little town. After a lifetime of watching communities from outside the circle, she was finally beginning to fit in with one. It hadn't been easy. She looked across the crowd of faces. Business owners, community leaders, and other professionals called greetings to each other. Most of them had lived in Wild Rose Ridge their entire lives. Many of them were related. Family ties ran strong.

You couldn't throw a stick in this town and not hit a Weaver, a Coleman, or a Walcott. Some, like the mayor, had family ties to all three. The fact that she, a newcomer of merely three years in the community, was about to be named the head of the play committee was a huge accomplishment. Becoming a town councilwoman later this summer would help even more. Not that she could consider the council spot an accomplishment. She was the only one who had volunteered to run for it when the earlier councilwoman had fallen ill and resigned.

She had Ivy to thank for all of it, though, for pulling her into this community and introducing her to everyone. She'd been the one to encourage her to go for the vacant city council spot. The tea and bookshop helped, of course. And the podcast. But joining the drama club had been her best decision yet.

Two years ago, she played a tiny part in the Wild Rose Day's play and became hooked. Then when Adele Langley, the former librarian, had asked her to help write the new script, she'd absolutely found her niche. Directing these past four months since Adele had left was so much fun.

An annoying screech, followed by the words, "Is this on?" came from the microphone at the front of the room. The age-old sign the meeting was about to start. Like the others in the room, Fiona took her seat and focused on their young mayor. Slowly, the talking in the room ceased.

"Welcome, everybody. Glad you could make it. As you all should know by now, the first wild roses were spotted up on Wild Rose Ridge. Thank you, Fiona, for the heads up." The mayor nodded her direction. "Sorry, it had to come at such a cost."

There you go—small-town living at its finest. Everyone knew everything about everyone's business. And, surprisingly, she loved it.

"No problem," she called back. "Glad to be of service."

Chuckles rippled through the room.

"So," Mayor Weaver continued. "The next order of business is planning this year's Wild Rose Days festival. The festival will officially start one week from this Saturday. Memorial Day Weekend falls then, bringing in extra visitors, so the timing is great."

Unless you were the parent of a college senior. But what would their single, thirty-something mayor know about that? Besides, graduation and end-of-the-year school events always came on the heels of the festival. It was all part of the hectic, crazy time they called spring. Wild Rose Ridgers were used to it by now. Whoever set the festival's timing all those years ago must have loved to live on adrenaline.

"Now, to set up the committees." Mayor Weaver continued. "Darlene Coleman will be in charge of booths and event organization again this year, so if you plan to have a booth for the festival, see her for location and fees."

The mayor looked up from his notes as the door at the back banged shut. "Ah, Chase. Glad you could finally make it."

Fiona turned in her seat, along with everyone else, to see a red-faced Chase standing in the doorway.

"Give a warm welcome to my cousin, Chase Coleman, folks. He's decided to come back home and join Doc Johnson's practice. If you're sick, be sure to give him a call."

The room erupted in applause. Chase gave a quick wave and flashed his million-dollar smile before finding a seat in the back row. Fiona was willing to bet that at least fifty percent of the women in the room had decided to get sick soon after seeing that smile. The other fifty percent were related to him, so they didn't count.

"Perfect timing there, cuz. We were getting ready to discuss the annual Wild Rose Days play. You were president of the drama club in high school, right? And played Jakob Jeremiah in the play your senior year? We happen to have a vacancy for play director and chair since Mrs. Langley retired and moved away."

Wait. What? Fiona didn't like the way this conversation was headed. The mayor should know she was the one Mrs. Langley had chosen to take her place. There was no vacancy. *She* was the committee's chair. *She* was the play director. The whole drama committee knew that.

"How about stepping in this year? Directing our play?" Arlan asked Chase.

"Um. Sure. I guess?"

This could not be happening. Fiona felt the stares of the drama club members and heard their whispers. "Wasn't Fiona–?" "Did she know–?" But, of course, this was happening. It always did.

Don't react. Don't let them see you cry. She'd had years of practice with these exact situations. Numerous times where she thought she was finally fitting in somewhere, only to realize she was, once again, inadequate.

She didn't have the connections, the history, the name. Had she honestly thought a committee chair would go to anyone other than a Coleman or a Morales or a Walcott in Wild Rose Ridge? Not unless she was related to one of them somehow. And she was related to exactly nobody in this room.

The side door beckoned. Suddenly, putting on a brave face didn't matter anymore. She needed to get out of there. Now. And who's to say she didn't need a bathroom break? Only two people sat between her and the end of the row. She could do this.

The mayor had moved on to a debate between him and Marla Mavis over publicity and a social media presence.

"Excuse me," she whispered to Katie Rose, who sat on her left. "I just need to . . ." Rising, she squeezed her way past Katie and then Jeremy, ignoring Ivy's attempt to grab her arm and the pain that shot down her thigh when the wound on her leg brushed against the chair in front of her. All she wanted was to get out that door and away from this crowd as quickly as possible. She'd deal with the fallout later.

Once she reached the sidewalk and started toward home, she let the tears fall. Wild Rose Ridge had rejected her once again. And once again, Chase was right in the center of that rejection.

Chapter Four

Could this day get any worse? Fiona set down her phone. Diane Alexander had canceled as a guest on her podcast today. Again. What was this now? Diane's third cancellation? Normally, when a guest canceled more than once, Fiona wouldn't reschedule them. But you didn't say no to the Alexanders, especially if they were your landlords.

She heaved a sigh. After staying up half the night downing ice cream and hashing out last night's fiasco with Ivy while fielding numerous texts from drama club members, Fiona was fried. She hadn't a peppy bone in her body this morning, no matter how many cups of Matcha tea, otherwise known as the Pippi Longstocking, she'd consumed. To make things worse, Ivy, her co-host, was elbow-deep in cupcake and cake frosting preparing for two major weddings this weekend. She couldn't make it today, either.

Sure, Fiona had done her podcast alone before. Usually, she had no trouble finding things to talk about while interacting with their faithful followers in the chat room. But not today. Not when she was wallowing in the depths of disappointment. She didn't have it in her.

Maybe she could get Benedict to sub for her today. She glanced over at her morose employee, who, as usual, sat behind the cash register with his head buried in a book. No. Benedict was a wizard at locating rare books and selling them on the Internet. A podcast host he was not. Fiona took another sip of her Matcha tea. Not her favorite flavor, but desperate times and all. Hopefully, its kick would hit her about the time she needed to go on air next hour.

Days like today were when her decision to change to a live format for her podcast came back to bite her. Normally, she loved the spontaneity and interaction the live podcast afforded. She and Ivy had built up a group of regulars on Tuesday mornings who were very active in their chat room. But having the luxury of airing a recorded show would have helped today.

The bookstore door jangled, and Chase Coleman walked in. Great. Just what she needed. Apparently, no amount of Matcha tea was going to be enough to turn this day around. She dropped to a crouch behind the bar, ignoring the pain in her stitched leg. Hopefully, he hadn't seen her. Maybe if she stayed down here, re-arranging tea bags long enough, he'd talk to Benedict about whatever it was he wanted.

"Hello."

She looked up to see his way-too-good-looking face peering down at her as he leaned across the bar. Drat.

"Hi."

"Catch you at a bad time?"

"No. Of course not. I was, um, organizing things." She cleared her throat and stood up, almost bumping his face as she rose. "What can I get for you?" She forced a smile. "Back for another Santiago?"

"No. I mean, it was good and all. I just had some coffee, though." He looked about as uncomfortable as she felt. Good. She hoped he was so uncomfortable he'd turn around and leave. "Actually, I came to talk to you about the play committee for the festival."

Uh, oh. Ivy must have talked to him. Or someone else from the drama club, even though she'd pleaded with all of them to let it go. Awkward notched up another level.

"What about it?"

"Jason told me you'd been directing the play the last few months, getting everyone ready."

Ah. Ivy's brother was the culprit. She was glad to know her friend hadn't betrayed her.

"And?"

"Well, I realize I'm coming in pretty late to the party." He raked a hand through his hair, leaving it looking honestly more attractive than before, if that was even possible. "The thing is, I don't know why Arlan put me in charge of the committee. Well, I kinda do. He said he wanted me to get involved in town events again. Said it would be good for business. Not that business in the health field is ever lacking, but PR-wise, I guess. Since I'm new and all. Anyway, I told him I'd be happy to help. I didn't expect him to make me a chairman of a whole committee." Chase was starting to look more uncomfortable than she felt. Good.

"Thing is, I don't mind being a part of the play committee. I liked drama in high school. A lot. But I don't have the time right now to give what would be needed as the chairperson. I thought maybe we could work together. Like co-chairs or something."

"Co-chairs?"

"Yeah. You give me all the jobs you don't want to do, you continue to direct the play, and we manage the thing together. What do you say?"

She looked into his deep chocolate eyes and knew she was a goner. He could be very persuasive when he wanted to be. Oh, who was she kidding? Chase Coleman could convince her to set herself on fire with no effort at all other than a flash of his killer grin. Besides, he offered her exactly what she wanted—a chance to direct the play.

"I say yes, under one condition." No need to let him see how badly she wanted this.

"What condition?"

"I'm guessing you don't have to be at work right away, given you are here chatting with me in the middle of a Tuesday morning?"

He flashed a crooked smile. Not the full kilowatt one, but still very effective. "You're right. The clinic is open from noon until eight p.m. on Tuesdays and Thursdays to accommodate those who can't get off work for appointments. Why?"

"Well, as it happens, I'm in need of a guest speaker on my podcast this morning."

"You have a podcast?"

"Yes. *Time for Tea with Fiona*. Ivy and I usually host together, but she's swamped with wedding orders this week. We start off talking about tea and books, but then we try to introduce a community member to help promote their business or an event they are planning. Today's guest had to cancel last minute, so we have an opening. It would be a perfect opportunity for you to reintroduce yourself to the Wild Rose community. PR-wise, you know."

"Tea and books?" His expression had a shade of panic to it.

"Just follow my lead on that part. It's mostly a conversation between the two of us. Then I'll interview you. Tell the community about you and your practice. It's more of a favor to you than it is to me. Though, you would be helping me out. Are you up for it?"

"If I do this, you'll agree to be my co-chair?"

"Absolutely. Deal?" She held out her hand.

"Deal."

She hadn't expected the tingle she felt when their hands touched. She should have. She'd always been way too aware of Chase Coleman. She gave his hand a quick shake, hoping he didn't notice how he flustered her.

"Good," she said, trying to sound normal. "We go on air in ten minutes. Oh, and I know you said you didn't want any tea, but you will need to drink at least a sip of today's flavor so we can discuss it."

He raised an eyebrow. "Who's on the menu today? Huckleberry Finn?"

She laughed. "No. But thanks for the idea. I could make a pretty good flavor with that name. I even know where I could get hold of some huckleberries."

"But . . . today's flavor?"

"You'll find out. Now, head on back to my studio. It's down the hall to the right." She pointed the way. "I'll grab the tea and two cups and be with you in a sec."

"Good morning, everyone. It's *Time for Tea with Fiona,* where we talk books, tea, and everything Wild Rose Ridge. I'm excited to have a special guest with us today who is no stranger to Wild Rose Ridge, Dr. Chase Coleman. He's graciously agreed to let me grill him today for our show, but before we get started, here's a word from our sponsors.

Fiona cued the advertising segment, then handed Chase his cup of tea. "Get ready to talk about your thoughts on this flavor when we get back on air."

"You want me to taste it now?"

"No. Wait until I tell you. I want your first impression to be without a lot of thought. Works better that way and feels more candid."

She switched off the cued tape and leaned into her microphone. "And we're back. Unfortunately, Ivy couldn't join us today. She's busy making all those cupcakes and wedding cakes for the Bricklin and McKnight weddings. Congratulations to the soon-to-be-married couples. There's no better place for a wedding than Wild Rose Ridge. And be sure to stop by Weaver's Bakery this week to say hi. While you're there, why not sample one of Vi's pies? Tell her Fiona sent you for a ten percent discount."

Fiona turned to Chase and pointed to his teacup. She

mouthed the word NOW and picked up her own cup. She'd purposely given Chase the most flowery teacup in her collection. The sight of him awkwardly holding it by its butterfly handle gave her just the satisfaction she'd been going for.

"It's time for our tea flavor of the week. I'm anxious to hear Dr. Coleman's thoughts on it. Go ahead, take a sip, doc, and tell us what you think."

Chase tentatively sipped, then sipped again. "Tastes like flowers."

"And?"

Chase sniffed at his cup and took another sip. "I don't know. Maybe some cream?"

Fiona laughed. "Folks, this is one time I wish we had a camera on this show so you could see the good doctor's face. I'm guessing this flavor will not be as popular with our male customers, but I know our ladies will love it. I give you the Elizabeth Bennet, or the Lizzy for short. A delightful English Rose blend of Ceylon black tea, rose buds, and petals. And as Dr. Coleman so quickly noted, it comes with a dash of English cream. Pair this flavor with a blueberry scone from Weaver's, and you can imagine yourself taking tea with Lizzy and Jane, dishing about all things Darcy and Bingley. The Lizzy will be on sale all week at Rosehips Tea and Books. Be sure to stop by and try a cup."

She picked up the papers she'd prepared for the show. "And now to our book portion of the show. Obviously, Elizabeth Bennet is the main character in Jane Austen's novel *Pride and Prejudice*. Austen began the novel in 1796 when she was only twenty years old.

However, she did not sell it to a publisher for another sixteen years after significantly revising it and changing its name from *First Impressions* to *Pride and Prejudice*. Over two hundred years later, it remains the most popular of all of Austen's books and has spawned numerous literary, movie, theater, and TV adaptations. Tell me, Dr. Coleman, have you read the book?"

"Uh. No."

"Seen any of the movies?"

"Again, no."

"Know anything about the book at all?"

"Other than what you just said? No. Oh, wait. I had a girlfriend in college who had to read it for some English class. She seemed to love it. It's mostly a girl book, right?"

"On this show, we don't discriminate between boy and girl books. We treat all books equally."

"I meant, it's a book that girls like more than guys do."

"We'll let our audience decide that. Your job today is to read these excerpts I've highlighted so our audience will get a taste of the glory that is *Pride and Prejudice*."

Chase raised his eyebrows at her as she passed him the sheet with the quotes.

"Start with those lines there—the quintessential first paragraph. Go ahead. Show us some of those drama skills we've heard so much about." Had that sounded sarcastic? Maybe a tad.

Chase gave her a weighted look, cleared his throat, and began. "'It is a truth universally acknowledged, that a single man in possession of a good fortune, must be in want of a wife. However little known the feelings or views of such a man may be on his first entering a neighbourhood, this truth is so well fixed in the minds of the surrounding families that he is considered as the rightful property of some one or other of their daughters.'"

Hmmm. He did have a nice reading voice. She'd be happy to listen to him all day. But she had an audience to satisfy. "So. What do you think?"

"About what?"

"The first lines."

"A little wordy."

"Anything else?"

"There's a dry humor to it. Witty."

"Does it make you want to read more?"

"Not really. She should start with a murder or a good chase scene. Then I'd be hooked."

"All the women in the audience, myself included, are shaking their heads at you, Dr. Coleman."

"And all the men are applauding. Am I right, guys?"

Fiona chuckled. "Maybe, but you're not off the hook yet. Read the next excerpt, please."

He read the section where Mr. Darcy insulted Elizabeth at the Meryton Assembly.

"Well, what do you think?"

"Ouch. Not a great start. But I bet they end up together in the end."

"What makes you say that?"

"Isn't that a common plot of a romance? First, they hate each other. Then, they love each other."

"Enemies to lovers is a common romance trope. Yes."

"So, they end up together."

"On this show, we do not give spoilers."

"You can't spoil the ending of a romance. It's a given.

Of course, they end up together. Besides, you said earlier that the book was written two hundred years ago and spawned all sorts of movies and plays. I'm sure anyone who wants to know knows the ending already."

"That may be, but we don't tell the ending of any book on this podcast. I *will* tell you that Lizzy receives at least two proposals in the story. In fact, why don't you go ahead and read the next two excerpts for us, and we'll discuss."

Chase obliged by reading first Mr. Collins's proposal to Lizzy, followed by Mr. Darcy's first proposal.

"Thoughts?"

"These dudes need some real work on their content and delivery. Did any one of those work?"

"No. But both men do end up engaged by the end of the book. I won't say who they get engaged to. Like I said, there will be no spoilers coming from me."

"And, like *I* said, the ending was spoiled the minute we realized it was a romance. Lizzy and Darcy end up together. End of story."

Fiona couldn't help laughing. "Other than that, what are your overall impressions of Austen and *Pride and Prejudice* in particular?"

"I'd say Austen has a sharp wit and does a good job creating relatable characters."

"Would you read the book?"

"Probably not. Unless it was required for a class or something. I think I'll stick to thrillers."

"Fair enough, but it might not hurt you to branch out a bit. Give a new genre a try now and then. Who knows? You might end up liking it. Now, to all you ladies out there, I know you are dying to hear all the deets on our handsome new doctor, but you'll have to wait until after these messages. Getting up close and personal with Dr. Coleman is next on our agenda. After the break."

She punched the cued recorded segment and turned to Chase. "That was good. You're not nearly as enthusiastic about *Pride and Prejudice* as Ivy would have been, but I think it's good to give our listeners a different perspective now and then."

Chase studied her, a half-smile on his face. "You think I'm handsome? You want to get up close and personal with me?"

Fiona felt the heat build on her face. Being a ginger had its disadvantages when it came to blushes. She knew from experience that everything from her neck up was a bright red right now, and it wasn't pretty.

"I said that as a teaser."

"Aw, now you're just a tease? I'm heartbroken."

"You know what I mean. It gets everyone to come back after our break, which—" She glanced at the stopwatch on her screen. "should be happening right about now."

Thank goodness. Things were getting entirely too hot in here.

"And we're back. As I said earlier, we are talking today with Dr. Chase Coleman, who has returned to Wild Rose Ridge and partnered with Dr. Johnson at our local clinic. I say 'returned' because you aren't new to the area, are you?"

"Nope. Born and raised here."

"Many of our listeners will know you as the son of

Rob and Darlene Coleman of Rose Cove Vineyards. Your family has owned and farmed land in this area for five generations. So, what got you interested in medicine instead of agriculture?"

"I was in a bad motorcycle accident my junior year of high school. I spent a lot of time in the hospital and then in physical therapy. Through that experience, I learned to appreciate all the medical field does to help people. I don't know. I guess I just wanted to be a part of that."

"You did your undergraduate work at Gonzaga University. Where did you go after that?"

"The University of Washington Medical Center, then a three-year residency in Seattle."

"And what brought you back to Wild Rose Ridge?"

"Who wouldn't want to live here, right? It's a sportsman's dream. Sailing, mountain biking, fishing, skiing. You name it. Wild Rose has it. And then there are the people. You couldn't ask for a friendlier, more welcoming place than Wild Rose Ridge."

"Especially if you're related to most of the town."

"Not most of them."

"Okay. Half of them, then."

"And, as I was saying, I've found all of them—even the ones I'm not related to—very friendly and welcoming. Long story short, I'm glad to be back."

His grin made her equally as glad he was back.

"In addition to your work at the clinic, what are your plans now that you are back in Wild Rose Ridge?"

"Well, I've been gone for schooling and residency for several years with very little time off, so I'm glad to have time to spend with my parents. Maybe even help my dad some out at Rose Cove. I may not have chosen agriculture as my career path, but I love spending time in the vineyards tending the grapes. There's something very soothing about working the land. We've recently added some new varietals and are making our own wine. It's fun to be a part of that."

"And you've jumped right into volunteering for town events. You're the chairman of the play committee for our upcoming Wild Rose Festival. How is that going?" Was she really going to go there? Apparently, she was.

"I have no idea since I was only appointed chair last night. But since you've so graciously agreed to be my co-chair on that committee, I would say it's going very well."

Darn. He was making her blush again.

"Rumor has it you played a mean Jakob Jeremiah back in the day."

He snorted. "Every male adolescent with the last name of Coleman has played Jakob Jeremiah. My brother Oliver . . . my cousin Jason . . . my dad . . . it's not a unique part. For Colemans, that is."

"But you were president of your high school drama team, right? I'm assuming you've had other parts over the years."

"Sure. I played Rolf in *The Sound of Music*, Gaston in *Beauty and the Beast*, and Curly in *Oklahoma* my senior year."

"Those are some pretty impressive roles. And all musicals. I'm guessing you can sing, then, as well as act?"

"Remember. This was Wild Rose Ridge High School, not Broadway. I sing well enough to get by."

"So, you won't be singing for us today?"

"Nope."

"Darn. Which role was your favorite?"

"Oh. Gaston, by far. There's nothing more fun than playing an over-confident, narcissistic villain."

"I'm surprised. I would have thought that Curly would have been more your cup of tea."

"Tea reference. Good one. Naw. Villains are by far the most fun to play."

"Well, there you have it, folks. The good doctor has a mean streak. You might want to think twice if he comes after you with a needle. Though I can speak from experience that he has very gentle hands." Did she just say that? Oh, Lord. "When it comes to stitches, I mean. And all the doctor-y things." She was only making it worse, and Chase was laughing out loud now. Time to wrap this up.

"And that's all the time we have for today! Be sure to visit Dr. Coleman and Dr. Johnson at the Wild Rose Ridge clinic for all your medical needs. Clinic hours are nine to five, Mondays, Wednesdays, and Fridays. Noon until eight p.m. on Tuesdays and Thursdays, and eight a.m. until noon on Saturdays. And remember, the secret to a well-balanced life is a cup of tea in one hand and a good book in the other. Until next time!"

She stopped the recording and shut the lid on her computer before turning to Chase. "Thanks for doing that. You're a lifesaver."

"Thanks for asking me. It was way more fun than I thought it would be." He glanced at the clock on her office wall. "But if that's the correct time, I better be going. The clinic opens in half an hour. Depending on appointments, I might be a little late to play practice. You can cover for me, right?"

"I'm sure we'll be fine." Since she'd been handling play practices for months without his help, she knew they would be. Her bigger worry was how things would go once he did show up.

Chase had barely left the tea shop when her phone buzzed. Ivy.

"What was that?!?"

"What?"

"The podcast. You and Chase were totally flirting."

"We were not. It was just friendly banter."

"That wasn't just friendly banter. I could feel the heat from here."

"You work in a bakery. Of course, you feel the heat."

"You know what I mean. 'Handsome doctor' . . . 'gentle hands' . . . Really? Not flirting? Tell me this. Did you blush even once during that interview?"

"Your point?"

"My point was made when you evaded that answer. But is what he said true? The two of you are going to co-chair the play committee?"

"Yes."

"How did that happen?"

"He asked. Apparently, Jason spilled the beans about me directing play practices over the winter."

"And Chase asked you to help?"

"Yep."

"You're sure nothing is going on between the two of you?"

"Strictly business."

"Yeah. We'll see how long that lasts. Hey, I gotta run. Customers are coming in for lunch. I'll see you tonight at play practice."

"See ya."

Fiona dropped her phone on the desk and buried her head in her hands. Had she just made a fool of herself in front of the whole town? Hopefully not. Ivy was always reading into things that weren't there. Chase Coleman hadn't been flirting with her. He was being friendly, nothing more. She'd made that mistake before. No way she was going to make it again. She'd keep things strictly professional between them tonight.

And from here on out.

Chapter Five

Chase let himself in the back door of the high school auditorium and tiptoed into the open area backstage. He was late. His last appointment had gone long. He sent a quick text to Fiona earlier but didn't receive a reply. Hopefully, she hadn't needed his help getting practice started. Oh, who was he kidding? She probably didn't need his help at all. She'd been in charge of this play and its actors all winter. He was coming late to the party. Literally and figuratively.

He stopped at the edge of the curtains and looked out onto the stage. How many times had he stood in this same spot waiting for his turn to go on? As he'd suspected, the play practice was already in full swing. A high school kid lounged a few feet away from him, his shoulder resting against one of the backstage props. He turned his head as Chase walked up and gave a nod. Probably, this year's Jakob Jeremiah. Not a Coleman relation, as far as Chase could tell, but he felt an instant bond with the guy. He nodded back, then directed his attention to the stage.

A spotlight was on a young girl seated on an enormous boulder at the front of the stage. She wrote in a diary while a girl's voice narrated from the speakers on each side of the stage. "I am not the only one in my family to make friends with the new homesteaders. Papa has struck up quite a friendship with Jakob's father. They meet almost as much as Jakob and I do."

The spotlight faded, and the girl slipped offstage to the opposite wing. The stage lights came up to show two men sitting on a bench under a large tree. The younger of the two wore his hair long, the ends just touching his shoulders. Chase recognized him as his tenth-grade biology teacher, Mr. Salinas. Max Hanford, who worked for ACRES real estate, sat beside him, chewing on a pipe.

Mr. Salinas held up three sticks wrapped in burlap. "You said you wanted to start an orchard on your homestead. I've brought you three apple tree cuttings to help you get started."

"They grow well here, then?"

"Apple trees grow very well in this valley, as well as pears and cherries. Trust me. I've had far more success farming this land than I ever had mining it."

"You've been here a long time, ya?"

"Only for the last sixteen years. But my wife's tribe has lived off this land for centuries. When President Cleveland said this land was open to all for homesteading, our family wasn't about to leave. I took the homestead the President offered, but this land was ours long before Chief Moses was given claim to it. No paper signed back east is going to change that."

"There is no land for us back in Deutschland. There

we worked in the Duke's vineyards but had no land of our own. I'm thinking of planting a vineyard here—a small one. Since you have shared your apple trees with me, I will share some vine cuttings with you. They come from the best vines in the world grown in the Württemberg Kingdom in Deutschland."

"We will plant our vineyard together, my friend. Right here by these trees. Maybe someday in the future, we will share a glass of wine here."

Wait. That isn't how the story went. Not according to Grandpa. And certainly not according to the original Wild Rose play. Someone had changed the script. Completely. When had this happened?

Chase strode out onto the stage.

"Hold on there, guys. That's not in the script I remember." For that matter, neither was the diary writing and narration. "Who made all these changes?"

"I did."

Chase turned toward the voice to find Fiona sitting in the front row, clipboard in hand.

"Why? The old script was fine."

"No, it wasn't. It was outdated and, in some parts, offensive to Native Americans. Mrs. Langley and I decided to write a new script after last year's performance."

"And the town was okay with that? It might be hokey, but the old script has been a Wild Rose Ridge tradition for decades."

"Didn't you even look over your copy of the play before coming to practice tonight?"

"I didn't think I'd need to. I know the play. Remember? I was in it. After all, it's been the same play since the town established Wild Rose Days back in the fifties."

"All the more reason for a change, don't you think?"

"No. I don't. And I'm pretty sure there will be a lot of townspeople who will agree with me."

Mr. Salinas, who stood right behind him on the stage, cleared his throat. "Um, Chase? You might want to give this new script a chance. It's good. Fiona and Adele put a lot of work into it. It feels more contemporary, and it's based a lot more on historical fact than the earlier one."

"Not the part I just saw. That's *my* family's history we're talking about here. I should know if it's fact or not. We never shared our vines with the Bouchard family. Ever."

An uncomfortable silence followed his outburst. Great. He hadn't meant to raise his voice. He wasn't making much of an impression as co-director, coming in late, and losing his cool. He turned to Fiona. "Maybe we could talk privately for a minute?"

She nodded. "Ivy, could you and Jeremy work on the blocking and lighting for the next scene while Chase and I take a minute to talk over the script?"

His cousin, who sat next to Fiona on the front row, gave him a where's-this-coming-from glare, then smiled at Fiona. "I'd be happy to."

Chase took the side steps off the stage and motioned for Fiona to follow him to the far side aisle of the auditorium, far enough away that the others wouldn't hear. As Fiona joined him, he was struck once again by her beauty. Her bright hair cascaded down her shoulders, framing her delicate features, but her eyes drew him the most.

He didn't know if he'd ever seen anyone with eyes quite that shade of blue. Growing up, he remembered his mom wearing a silky, deep-blue dress she called indigo blue. He'd thought that dress was the most beautiful color he'd ever seen. The word indigo had stuck with him ever since. Fiona's eyes were like that dress. They looked at him now with more than a hint of agitation.

He raked a hand through his hair. "I'm sorry. I should never have argued with you in front of everyone. I want us to be a united front when it comes to directing this play. Only . . . I wasn't expecting to see an entirely different play. Do any of the townspeople, besides those in the play, know about all the changes you made? I know my mom never mentioned it, and neither did Arlan. Do they know, at least? As the ones in charge of the whole festival, they probably should."

Fiona's perturbed look faded to worry. "Honestly, I don't even know. When Adele Langley came to me after last year's play to talk about re-writing the script, I thought she had the right to do so. Of course, I also thought she'd told Arlan that I was to be her successor on the committee, so . . ." Her words trailed off. "Do you think there will be pushback from the community?"

"I don't know. I mean, maybe? I can't be the only one who sees this play as a town tradition."

"It's essentially the same storyline, for the most part. But this version is not based so much on myths as it is on true history. Rose's dance studio will still perform the

Wild Rose Romeo-and-Juliet-style story. Ours is based more in reality."

"Whose reality? Hey, I'm all about dropping the teen suicide portion of it. Everyone knows my great, great, whatever grandfather never died on Wild Rose Ridge. Otherwise, I wouldn't be here. But that part about us giving the Bouchard family our vines in friendship? Hogwash. They stole those vines from us. Ask my father and his father. How else would those heritage Lemberger vines all have ended up on their property with none of them on ours? Our family came from the Württemberg region of Germany. Not theirs."

"I don't know the answer to that, but I do know that everything Adele and I wrote into the play's script is based on documented historical facts. We made sure of it. Maybe I should explain why we wanted to change the play in the first place. I know the town feels a sense of ownership of the old play, but they are not the only ones who watch it. Thousands of tourists visit the town every year to participate in the Wild Rose Festival. You know as well as I do that our population doubles, even triples, during the summer tourist season, and this festival kicks everything off.

"Well, right after the festival last year, there was an article in the *Seattle Times* criticizing Wild Rose Ridge for perpetuating racist themes and stereotypes by continuing to perform the play year after year. In a way, the writer was right. The Native American characters in the original play were all written using 1950s American stereotypes. The term Redskins was used a total of fifteen times during the play. The Native American characters weren't anything more than one-dimensional figures."

"That could be said of the white characters as well." Chase shrugged. "It wasn't a prize-winning script. It was probably cobbled together by a group of middle-aged housewives who decided it would be fun to tell the town's history in the form of a play for Wild Rose Days."

"Exactly. Adele thought we could do better, especially after she found Tehya's diary."

"Who the heck is Tehya?"

"Indian Rose. Or at least, that's what she was called in the first play."

"She actually existed?"

"Yes. She's as real as your great, great, great grandparents. Look, I'd like to tell you all about our research and how we found the material we used for this version of the play, but we've got a stage full of actors who expect to make some serious progress during rehearsal tonight. Could we finish this talk later?"

"All right. How about tonight after practice?"

"Practice is supposed to run another hour. Won't that be too late for you?"

He'd had an early morning and a long day, but he wasn't about to let that hinder his spending more time with her.

"I'm just coming off three years of residency. I'm used to going weeks without more than a couple of hours of sleep a night. One late night isn't going to kill me. You go ahead and run tonight's practice. I'll sit over here and watch and not say a word. I promise."

"Well, since you *are* co-director, it might be even

better if you join me in the front row. I'll even give you a notepad to jot down any changes or suggestions you'd like to make in the scenes you watch tonight. We can discuss those after the rehearsal too."

"I can do that. And Fiona, thanks for putting up with my outburst. I promise to keep an open mind."

"Thank you for listening. I think once you see the whole play, you will like it."

He hoped so. It was getting harder and harder to say no to those blue eyes.

Chase bit into his slice of pepperoni and sausage pizza and looked out across Wild Rose Lake. Summer nights like this brought back so many childhood memories. In fact, nights like this were a big part of why he decided to make Wild Rose Ridge his home. Though it was late, the light had not completely faded from the sky. If he looked way off in the distance over Mount Raven, he could see the first stars. Soon the sky above would be covered with them, hanging low and bright in the cool night air. How many times had he sat at this very spot and watched them over the years?

Not enough, lately. Not nearly enough.

He grabbed another slice of pizza and turned to the girl next to him. "Ah. Eating Crusty's Pizza on the dock. Sure brings back memories."

Fiona laughed. "I might have had a few slices with Ivy back in the day, now that you mention it. Probably not as often as you, from the sounds of it."

"I worked construction for my uncle during high school. Late-night pizza on the dock was a common theme of my summer workdays. You were here a few summers, right?"

"Just three. My sixth through eighth-grade years. We were living in Twin Falls, Idaho, for those years. My dad's dad was pretty sick with cancer. My parents had come back to the states to be closer to him while he went through his treatments. I spent summers with my grandparents on my mom's side."

"That's right. They had a house next to Jason and Ivy's. Do they still own it?"

"No. They passed away during my senior year of college. Both of them. Within three months of each other. Pop Pop passed first of a heart attack, and a few months later, Mimi died in her sleep. We figure she didn't want to be without Pop Pop any longer. They always did everything together. You'd never see one without the other. So . . ." Her words trailed off. A sadness shrouded her posture.

"Yeah. It's hard to lose grandparents. Grandpa Ben died eight years ago, and I still miss him. I always expect to see him when I'm walking through the vineyards, bent over some vine or messing with a tractor."

Fiona nodded. "Mimi and Pop Pop are the reason I have the bookstore. They left me their lake house. After college, I came back to see what to do with it and ended up staying. I sold the house and bought the inventory for the bookstore and tea shop with it. Right now, I'm renting the building and the apartment above it, but I wouldn't mind buying it someday if the Alexanders would ever consider selling."

"Good luck with that. They own practically half of downtown and seem to like being landlords."

"I've noticed. Last week, they sent out a letter notifying us of a rate increase. Thankfully, our internet sales of antique books and first-editions are doing well. Benedict is a bloodhound at nosing those out for us. I don't know what I'd do without his expertise."

That explained the purpose of the morose-looking young man behind the cash register. He hadn't thought the man had been hired for his great customer service. The few times Chase had been in Fiona's shop, he hadn't seen him look up from his book.

"So, tell me about how the new script came about. You said there was an article in the *Seattle Times?*

Fiona nodded. "The week after last year's festival. It was an opinion piece by Jessica Hudson, a Native American journalist. She had picked up on an article in our town's *Remarkable News* that had criticized the play and came to see it. Both articles had some valid points, as I mentioned earlier. The town didn't like the negative publicity much. Hudson called us racist and provincial. That's why Adele came up with the idea of re-writing it. That, and Tehya's diary."

"You found a diary?"

"Yes, all of the play's narration is actual excerpts from it."

"I had no idea the Indian girl was a real person. I thought she was someone the town founders made up to make our history sound a little more interesting. I'm glad you expanded the part for Gertrude Schulte in your revision. She was nothing more than a mention in the first one, which I always thought was a slap in the face to my great-great whatever grandmother. There must not have been any Colemans or Schultes on the first play committee for them to have left her out altogether."

Fiona laughed. He liked the sound of her laugh.

"Think about it," he said. "The woman birthed seven children to Jakob Jeremiah. You'd think she deserved more than a mere mention. This version brings her to life. Shows her as more than simply an off-screen villain who tore two star-crossed lovers apart."

"Adele and I tried to make this play more realistic. We delved pretty deeply into the character's emotions and goals. I hope that comes across in the performance."

"I think it will. From what I saw tonight, this play is light-years better than the first one. The girl who plays Tehya is very talented. I think we'll have a hit on our hands."

"You weren't so sure about that earlier this evening. What happened to the town not wanting its traditions messed with?"

"You'll probably still run into a fair amount of that. I'm sure I'm not the only one who values the traditions of this town, but having seen the whole play, or at least most of it, I think you can win over the traditionalists too. There's still enough of the storyline intact to satisfy all of us."

"Well, that's good to hear. We were trying to mitigate controversy, not stir it up."

"Is that even possible these days? Kudos to you if you can pull it off. But the part I'm most interested in is the scene I walked in on between Mr. Bouchard and Papa

Kohlmann. You said all your scenes are based on historical facts, but according to my grandfather, our family never shared anything with the Bouchard family. How all the clones from the historic Württemberg vines ended up on the Morales property is one big mystery. You say you have proof they were shared?"

"A few of them, yes. It was in Tehya's diary. I don't remember the exact wording, a simple line or two at most, but she said something about her father and Jakob's father planting a small vineyard on either side of their property line. Maybe, through the years, the only ones to survive were the ones on the Morales property."

"Where did you find the diary? The Indian princess portrayed in the first play could barely speak English, let alone read and write."

"That's the beauty of finding Tehya's diary. We learned so much more about that family than we ever knew before. Apparently, Tehya's mom was the daughter of the Indian chief, Tall John, whose family had lived on these shores for centuries. She had married a French-Canadian named Bouchard, who had come into the area with a logging company. They had three sons older than Tehya, but she was their only daughter. She was much younger than the other children, and her father doted on her. He sent her to a convent school in his hometown in Canada, where she learned to read and write. She was fluent in French and English, as well as Salishan. Papa Bouchard had big plans for her that all came crashing down when she became pregnant out of wedlock. He was furious when Papa Kohlmann didn't think she was good enough for his son."

"You got all that from her diary?"

"That and the letters."

"What letters?"

"The packet of love letters I found tucked in a trunk from your great, great-aunt Edith's estate. One of the services Bernard and I provide is helping people go through their loved ones' estate papers and books to see if there are any of value. We help them decide what to keep and what to give away. Your aunt hired me when her great-aunt Edith died. I found the packet of letters wrapped in twine and buried beneath a bunch of papers in an old box. They were letters Tehya had written to Jakob. I'm guessing he also wrote back, but we never found those, of course. They would have been in Tehya's possession. They did help us authenticate Tehya's diary, though. Same handwriting. Same voice."

"You never did tell me where you got the diary."

"Oh, that's right. Well, shortly after that letter appeared in The Seattle Times, Adele Langley asked me if I wanted to help her rewrite the play. She knew I'd been dabbling in script writing and told me she might have some material to help improve the play. She showed me Tehya's diary. Apparently, it had been sent to her from the library on the Yakama Indian Reservation, along with other books and papers that had some connection with Wild Rose Ridge. When she realized what it was, she thought immediately of the play and knew it would be great primary source material. Finding the letters a few months later was a godsend. We knew we had to rewrite the play more accurately. Tehya's story deserved to be told."

Chase could hear the passion in Fiona's voice. "You really love history, don't you?"

"I love stories. Past and present. Maybe that's why I sell books."

"And write amazing plays."

He was rewarded with another laugh. He set aside the pizza box and lay back on the dock. While they'd been talking, the stars had come out in all their summer glory.

"Have you ever looked at the stars from this dock?"

"No, I wasn't allowed to be out that late back then."

As he had hoped, she lay down next to him.

"You've missed out then. Look. Right up there." He pointed to the north over Mount Raven. "You can see the Big Dipper. One Native American legend called it Fisher. The story goes that a great hunter named Fisher once climbed into Skyland to bring back summer for his people. He was caught letting the warm winds escape from their baskets. The Sky People filled him with arrows as he ran, and he died. As he fell from the sky, his body was turned into stars. Sometimes you see him falling on his back. Sometimes he's turned onto his feet."

She turned her head toward him and smiled. He could see the white of her teeth in the semi-darkness. "You like stories too. Admit it."

"I guess I do. Maybe that was why I was drawn to the drama club in high school."

"You were good at it."

"How would you know that?"

"Ivy posted a video of you on Facebook once. You

were singing 'Oh, What a Beautiful Morning' from *Oklahoma.*"

"Well, that's embarrassing."

"Not at all. You did a great job."

Time to change the subject. "So you go through papers and books for estate sales? Do you ever go through them for people before they die?"

"Sometimes. If people want to downsize or move away. I helped Adele before she moved to San Diego."

"Could I hire you?"

"You seem a bit young to have a large collection."

"Not me so much. But my parents."

"They aren't moving, are they?"

"No. But they have an attic stuffed with generations worth of old things. There must be papers and books up there too. Who's to say there aren't more letters or documents that could help tell us more about our family's story? That scene between Jacques Bouchard and Wilhelm Kohlmann is still bugging me. Grandpa Ben always insisted our vines were stolen. What if we could find proof one way or the other? Grandpa Ben and my dad have always been so bitter about the fact that those vines passed out of our family. I'd just like to know the truth. Would you help me? You'd have a better idea of what we'd need to look for."

She was quiet for so long that he thought she would say no. But, finally.

"Sure, I'll help you. But you don't need to pay me. Consider it a friend helping a friend unless we find a valuable book or two. Then you can pay me a commission for selling them." She hesitated a minute. "We are friends, right?"

He turned his head to look at her. Her face was mere inches from his, her eyes dark pools in the dusky light. He allowed himself to reach over and trace a finger down her silky cheek.

"To be honest, I'm kinda hoping we can be more than friends."

The slightest of smiles gave him all the encouragement he needed. He slowly leaned over and pressed his lips to hers. He could taste the saltiness of the pizza on her lips. Tentatively, he explored the shape of her mouth.

With a soft sigh, she responded, kissing him back. He pulled her closer, deepening the kiss. Abruptly, she tore away from him and sat up.

"It's getting late," she said. "I should go."

Before he even had a chance to respond, she was up and heading toward the other end of the dock. Was it something he did? Well, of course, it was something he did. He shouldn't have kissed her. Not yet. Not like that, anyway. He was rushing things. They'd only known each other for three days. But here he was, diving in way too fast. Getting in way over his head.

He'd promised himself he'd never do that again. Jump into a relationship way too soon. And he wouldn't. He'd take things slow. Be her friend first. He could do that. He could. Except, after the kiss they'd just shared, he couldn't quite keep himself from wanting more.

Chapter Six

That kiss! She didn't know what to make of it. She had dreamed of kissing Chase Coleman for so long, she still wasn't sure whether it was fiction or reality. No. It was definitely reality. Her dreams had never concocted a kiss that good. Yet here she was four days later, and she still didn't know what that kiss was all about.

It was all her fault. She totally knew that. Because after that wonderful, delicious, earth-shattering kiss, she'd panicked. She had said something lame like, "look how late it's getting," and took off like a scared little rabbit. Since then, neither of them had mentioned the kiss.

She'd seen Chase every night since then at play practice, and they both acted as if that kiss had never happened. They'd discussed timing, blocking, lighting, play promotion, and everything play-related, but nothing, NOTHING, about that kiss. He hadn't asked her to any more late-night pizza sessions on the dock either. Probably never would. Ugh. Why did she have to be such a dork?

And now, in less than two hours, she was meeting him at his parent's house to search through attics with him. Just the two of them. Alone. With that kiss and her reaction to it hanging between them like a bright red pimple on the end of a nose. The more you didn't want to look at it, the larger it grew.

Maybe she should call him and tell him she was sick. No. You can't lie to a doctor about being sick. He'd see right through it. An emergency here at the store, then. Surely, she could think of something.

No. She wasn't going to play that game. She told him she'd help him, and she would. She could tell that finding that information for his family was important to him. She wasn't going to let him down. Awkward as it may be, she also needed to clear up whatever this was between them. She owed it to herself and to him not to run away. Had he meant it when he'd said he wanted to be more than friends? Had she read something into that kiss that wasn't really there?

Because, if he had meant it, why hadn't he brought it up again? Made some effort to talk to her alone? Maybe he hadn't meant it. Maybe he'd been caught up in the moment. The stars. The lake. The late-night conversation. Oh, land's sake. She needed to get over herself and just ask him. Before she could lose her courage, she took one last look at herself in the mirror, grabbed her keys, and headed down the back stairs to her car.

She'd hired Katie Rose Lilly from the drama club to be her tea barista this summer. With her in the tea shop and Benedict manning the books, she shouldn't need to be back until two. Plenty of time to explore the Coleman attics. She knew perfectly well that the nervous energy coursing through her had less to do with what they might discover in the attics and much more with the handsome doctor who would be helping her. Still, she'd always enjoyed a good treasure hunt.

As she drove through town and up toward the Ridge where the Coleman and Morales vineyards were located, she wished more than ever that she hadn't panicked and run after Chase kissed her. She was a grown woman, a business owner, and a totally capable adult, but when it came to Chase, she reverted to that thirteen-year-old girl who'd made an utter fool of herself over him.

Thank goodness, he never noticed the depths of her foolishness that summer. At sixteen, he'd never really noticed her at all. She knew that now. She wished her thirteen-year-old self had been smart enough to know it. It would have saved her a lot of heartache.

As she drove along Rose Lake Boulevard, she glanced toward the marina where her greatest humiliation had occurred. It wasn't that far from the dock where their kiss had taken place. The two events melded together now. She wondered if Chase even remembered the first time they'd sat on that dock together, just talking. It had always been a red-letter day in her memory. It probably wasn't even a blip on his radar. She could almost see her thirteen-year-old self sitting on the end of that dock, legs swinging above the water, watching Chase fish and talking a mile a minute. She was always talking back then. She'd learned to choose her words more carefully these days, but back then, she pretty much let everyone know what she was thinking every minute of the day, whether they wanted to listen or not.

That particular day she had Chase all to herself, and surprisingly, he hadn't seemed to mind. He would even laugh now and then at something she'd said, encouraging her to talk even more. And then, when she'd gotten up to leave, knowing her grandparents were expecting her for dinner, he'd said, "Hey, Princess. I'm thinking of sailing over to the island tomorrow. How'd you like to come with me? Jason and Arlan both have to work. What do you say? You could be my first mate."

She'd thought she'd died and gone to heaven. Finally, Chase Coleman was noticing her. He wanted to spend the day with her. He wanted her to be his first mate!

She'd dressed so carefully that next day, choosing her favorite pair of shorts and a halter top neither her mother nor grandmother approved of. She had borrowed it from Ivy and sneaked out of the house before Mimi could see her. She'd even curled her hair. In her mind that day, she'd been all grown up. In actuality, she'd been a scrawny kid—all elbows and legs with eyes too big for her face. She'd even worn braces back then. She shuddered simply thinking about it.

The morning had started off so well. Chase had been at his sailboat like he'd promised and had taken her bag from her as she climbed aboard. She was sitting in the bow, watching him rig the sails when disaster walked up. Portia Morales, captain of the cheerleading squad, and her covey of cheerleading cronies sashayed down the dock like it was a model's runway. Portia was a senior, a year older than Chase. All the girls wore bikinis, but Portia filled hers out better than any of them. She climbed on board the sailboat and placed a hand on Chase's bare bicep.

"Hey, sailor," she said. "Any chance you can give my girls and me a ride to the island today? Arlan said you were going."

Chase turned to putty in her hands. "Sure," he'd stammered, actually stammered. Then his face fell. "But the boat only holds five people."

"Perfect," Portia purred. "The four of us and you."

"Yeah, but I promised Fiona she could come today."

All eyes had turned to her.

"The kid? Surely you can't be serious. You can take her anytime. But all of us need to go today. We're planning to take our informal cheer squad pictures over there. Arlan said you would help us out. You don't mind, do you, Fiona?"

"What do you say, squirt? Can we make it a rain check?" Chase had asked.

Squirt! She'd been proud of herself. She hadn't shed a tear until she made it to the parking lot. There'd never been a rain check, though. After that day, Portia and Chase became a couple. And after that summer, Fiona never returned to Wild Rose Ridge. Until three years ago, of course. But she couldn't help wondering if she was doing it again. Reading more into that kiss than she should have. That's why she hadn't dressed up a bit for this day. She'd worn her usual leggings and a t-shirt and plaited her hair into its usual braid. Put on minimal makeup.

She wasn't getting her hopes up again. Not where Chase was concerned. Not this time.

∼

Ten minutes later, Fiona drove up to the Coleman home. The two-story, white farmhouse with the wrap-around porch sat about halfway up the ridge, nestled amongst rows and rows of grapevines. The view from the porch looking down toward the lake could rival pretty much any view in Wild Rose Ridge. If they ever converted to a winery and offered a tasting room, the crowds would flock here just for the view.

Chase opened the door on her first ring, his trademark grin looking a tad relieved. Maybe she wasn't the only one to feel the awkwardness in their relationship since that kiss. She could only hope they could move past it, or today could be a very long day.

He ushered her into the house's open kitchen/dining area, where his mother was busy rifling through the contents of a large box. She'd been inside Darlene and Rob's house before when she spoke to Darlene's book club about identifying and collecting first editions. The old farmhouse had been updated in a modern farmhouse design. Its mahogany floors gleamed against the lighter grays and whites of the walls and trim. Navy accents were scattered throughout the decor. Unlike her first visit, where everything was pristine, today, every available flat surface was littered with boxes and tubs. Pamphlets and charts cluttered the large, rustic dining room table.

"Fiona," Darlene said. "I'm so glad you could come today. Please excuse the mess. One more week before the festival, and then all this goes away. Until then, I'm afraid my house is chaos central."

"A controlled chaos, I would imagine. The festival is no easy task to organize, but you always manage to pull it off beautifully."

"Bless you, girl. That's so sweet of you to say. How are you doing? Chase told me about your accident last week. Is your leg healing well?"

"I think so. It's getting pretty itchy, but otherwise, things look good."

"Which reminds me," Chase broke in. "You should probably call for an appointment some day next week, so we can get those stitches taken out."

Great. One more awkward event to add to their list of awkward encounters.

"And the play is going well?" Darlene asked.

"Yes. It's shaping up. Like you, though, I'll feel a lot better when this week is done, and the festival is underway. We've been leading up to this for a long time, it seems."

"Chase tells me I'm going to like the changes you and Adele made to the play. It was long overdue if you ask me. I was so excited when Adele told me she had enlisted your help re-writing it."

Fiona shot Chase a grateful look. He'd been very busy the last few days getting the word out on the play and letting key community members know there would be changes. His mother was not the least of them. She was glad to know Darlene had been on board the whole time.

"I do hope you like it. It was fun digging into Tehya's diary and using it to flesh out the history in the play."

"And you and Chase hope to find more history up in our attic?"

"Your family's history, for sure. If that's all right with you."

"Oh, I'm all for it. I've meant to get that attic sorted since we moved in here. But Oliver arrived shortly after that, and between raising my kids and helping Ben and Rob with the office part of the business, I never found the time. I'm afraid we've added more items to the mess up there than we've cleaned. Out of sight, out of mind, I guess. You'll see."

Leaving Darlene to her tubs of festival gear, Fiona followed Chase up a steep back staircase to the third-level attic. When he opened a door to the room that ran the length of the house, she did see. The room was stuffed from one end to the other with boxes, furniture, and everything in between. An old summer hat dangled from an antique mirror. A baseball glove and a partially deflated basketball lay discarded on the floor in front of her. An old guitar and a music stand leaned against one wall.

"This could take months to sort through," Fiona said.

Chase looked rueful. "Yeah. Sorry. I guess I haven't been up here in a while. I had no idea it was this bad."

"That's okay. I don't mind a treasure hunt. Do you have any idea where we should start looking for the information you want to find?"

"I'm guessing the farther back in the room we go, the better. Most of this stuff up here are things Oliver, Tori, and I used." He picked up an old leg brace and looked it over.

"Yours?"

"Yeah. Brings back some tough memories."

"The accident you talked about the other day on the podcast?"

He nodded. "The motorcycle accident. Thanksgiving of my junior year in high school."

She'd known about the accident. She was back in Kenya by that time, desperately trying to forget about her crush on Chase after that sailboat debacle. But she kept in touch with Ivy through Facebook and What's App. Ivy had given her hourly updates on Chase's condition for several weeks until he pulled out of the worst of it. At first, they thought he might die from his injuries. And she had thought she might die with him. Nope. She'd never quite gotten over that crush. She'd simply suppressed it.

She looked at him, pain etched across his handsome face, and wished she could pull him into her arms. Comfort him from the memories that still looked fresh and hard.

"Must have been a really tough time."

"Yeah." He gave his head a shake and set the brace down. "But that's water under the bridge now. Let's see what we can find up here, shall we?"

"Lead the way."

They threaded their way through the room, the items getting older the further back they went. This attic was like taking a walk through history, starting in the present day and going back, decade by decade. Boom boxes gave way to transistor radios and record players. Near the back of the room, Fiona spotted an upright, crank-operated phonograph that had to be over a hundred years old. It was as if the Colemans had packed the large room with memories one generation at a time. No one had bothered to go through the previous generation's stuff. They just added their own. This was what it looked like to have deep roots in one place. She'd never known anything like it.

Her childhood had been filled with moves. About the time she had become comfortable in one spot, they'd uprooted and moved to another. She'd learned not to keep too many possessions. Maybe that's why she was so fascinated with other people's stuff—the things they treasured and eventually left behind.

"This place is amazing," she said. "Have you ever considered donating some of the older items to the town museum? Wilbur Hanford, our town historian, would be salivating if he saw all this."

"To be honest, I haven't been up here in years. I doubt my parents have either. We might mention it to Mom but not until after the festival." He grinned. "She'd have my head if I brought up another project with all she's dealing with now."

"There's no hurry. These things have been here a while. Won't hurt for them to wait a little longer. It would be great to share some of them, though, rather than hide them away. I mean, look at this." She held up a brown wool hat with an eagle, globe, and anchor insignia on the front. "Isn't this an army hat?"

Chase took it from her, an expression of near reverence on his face. "Marines. World War I. I didn't know this was up here. It belonged to my great, great grandfather's brother Ellis. He died in the Battle of Belleau Wood. One of the Devil Dogs. I did a report on him back in school. I've seen a picture of him in the hat, but I never knew we had the real thing in this attic. What I wouldn't have given to have had this back then for show and tell."

"See? Museum material. No reason to keep all these things hidden."

"You're right. Uncle Ellis deserves to be known." With visible reluctance, Chase placed the hat back on the bookcase where Fiona had found it, then looked around. "We should be getting close to the time frame we're wanting. One generation away, at least. What should we be looking for?"

"Books and papers mostly. Anything that might look like a diary or business ledger would be helpful. I'll check the books in this bookcase. Why don't you check the drawers of that desk over there? Also, look in boxes and trunks. Anything that looks like it might hold old documents."

She lifted the first door on the old barrister bookcase and scanned the titles. Pulling out one entitled *The Flaming Sword*, she read the inscription on the flyleaf: *Ellis, From Evie, Christmas 1915*. Ellis. The same Ellis who died a few years later in France? And who was Evie? An aunt? A sister? She ran her fingers across the page, thinking as she always did of the other fingers that had done the same before her.

"Do you think your family would be interested in

selling any of these?" she asked. "Some of these books could be worth some money."

"You think? I can't imagine they'd be worth much."

"You never know. You can get anywhere from two to eight hundred dollars sometimes, depending on the book and its condition. First editions are especially valuable."

Chase gave a low whistle. "You're kidding. Do you see any there that look promising?"

"The whole bookcase looks promising. Most of these are over a hundred years old. The bookshelf itself is a valuable antique. Seriously, if your family ever needed to make some money, they're sitting on a treasure trove up here. Benedict is great at tracking down buyers, so let me know if you think they might want to sell some."

They worked in silence for a while, digging into boxes and searching through a few old trunks. A box full of farming ledgers from the early 1900s gave her hope but offered no new insight into property lines or the origin of the vineyard. Fiona sat back on her heels after rummaging through another box of books. They'd reached the back end of the attic and had yet to find items from the earliest generation of Colemans. Maybe they weren't here. For all they knew, those memories may have been divided amongst earlier family members and were sitting in someone else's attic, like those letters she'd found in Edith Coleman Richardson's estate papers.

"Could the farm documents have been stored somewhere else? Does your family have an office for their business where they might be?" She asked.

"I doubt it. Mom is in charge of that area. She organized all that years ago when she and Dad were first married. She took over the books and office work when Grandpa Ben realized how good she was at making order out of chaos. The only reason this area hasn't been sorted through is that she hasn't found the time yet. Just wait. If I tell her about some of the things we found up here, I'm betting this will be her summer project."

Fiona almost hoped that wasn't true. This room told a story. The story of a family with deep roots and a multitude of branches. Even though she had encouraged Chase to consider donating and selling some of the items, it felt wrong somehow to break up the story and send it in diverse directions.

She sighed. She'd always been far too sentimental about family heirlooms. They were just things, really. And they were doing no one any good hidden away up here. She looked around to make sure they weren't missing anything and spied something partially blocked by the headboard of an old crib. Knowing how the anatomy of these old attics worked, they might not be done yet.

"Hey," she called to Chase. "There's a short door over here. Do you think more things might be stored behind that knee wall?"

Chase looked to where she was pointing. "Only one way to find out."

Crouching below the roof line, he cleared a path to the small door and pulled the crib headboard out of the way. The door stuck on his first pull but yanked open when he put more force behind it. He poked his head inside.

"Whoa. You're right. This place is packed."

Fiona made her way over to him and crouched down beside him, catching a whiff of his cologne as she did. They'd been working together all morning, but this was the closest she'd been to him. She didn't mind his proximity at all. It took all her willpower not to lean closer and sniff his neck. Nice, Fiona. Way to be professional.

"Do you think we'll find the older stuff in there?" Chase turned to look at her, his face mere inches from her.

Fiona struggled to focus on his question and not on his lips. She cleared her throat and turned to peer into the dark space in front of her. "I'd bet on it. They probably used this main room as living space back then. This section behind the knee wall was probably their original storage area."

"Makes sense. Jakob and Gertrude did have seven children. They all had to sleep somewhere."

"When was the house built?"

"In the early 1900s. It's seen its share of remodels over the years. I'm guessing that as the families got smaller, this area became storage. It gets pretty hot up here in the summers."

It was feeling a little warm right now with Chase pressed so close to her. She couldn't quite keep her focus off the memory of that kiss. Why hadn't he said anything about it? Had it been that bad? Was it something he did with all the girls and therefore not at all memorable? She licked her lips, gathering the courage to broach the subject somehow, when he pushed forward and stuck his head deep into the crawl space.

"I don't think there's any way both of us will fit in

here. Should we pull something out to see if we have the right time period?"

Fiona tried to peer around his broad shoulders. "Is there something small? If not, I might be able to crawl in there. Do you have a flashlight I can use?"

Chase backed out of the opening. He pulled out his phone and put it on flashlight mode, pointing the beam into the crowded space. "It looks like there's an old trunk to the left of us. You could probably squeeze in there, but I'm not sure you can move it by yourself."

Squeezing past Chase, Fiona crawled into the narrow space and over to the battered, metal steamer trunk tucked up against the eaves. The age looked about right and there by the latch... initials.

"This looks promising. Initials JJK. Your family spelled its name with a K back then, right?"

"Yes, up until World War I. Ellis changed it when he joined the Marines. He didn't want to be confused for a Kraut if he signed up to fight them. The rest of the family did the same after he died. To honor him."

Fiona lifted the latch on the trunk and peered in. Pushing aside some clothes, she spied some books, a photo album, and a stack of ledgers. Bingo.

"I think we've found what we're looking for. Or at least as close as we're going to get. Do you think you could pull it your way if I push the other end? I don't think I'll be able to tell what all we have here until we get it out in the open."

After a lot of maneuvering and straining on her part to get the trunk into a position where Chase could grab it, he easily pulled it out of the crawl space and into the main room of the attic. What do you know? His muscles were not simply there for her to stare at. They served a greater purpose, it seemed.

She pulled out the first farm ledger and opened it up. January 1927 through December 1929. Still too late date-wise, but there was a whole stack of them. Maybe some of the earlier ones would be of help. If not, maybe there would be more trunks like this one packed back in that crawl space. Ones that belonged to Jakob Jeremiah's father. At least they were getting closer.

The alarm on Fiona's phone chimed. Darn.

"I'm going to have to call it quits. Bernard's shift is up in thirty minutes, and I'll need to get back to the store. Any chance I could take some of these books and ledgers with me? I could look through them tonight after the shop closes. See if I can find anything."

"Don't we have play practice tonight?"

"Right. But after that." She hated to stop now. They had barely gotten started, and these family records and books were beckoning her. She had the feeling she always had when uncovering a family's history. Giddy. There was no other word for it, and she hated to have to wait another week or more to dig into the treasures in this trunk. "I'd only take the books and get them back to you as soon as possible."

"That's no problem. I hate to have you work this hard when you're so busy with everything else."

"Trust me. It's not work. It's what I do for fun."

He studied her a moment, thoughts unreadable, before flashing her one of his killer grins.

"Okay. We'll get you loaded up then. I think I saw some empty boxes back by the steps when we came up."

Ten minutes later, Chase stacked two heavy boxes of ledgers and books into the trunk of her car, then came around and opened her door as she climbed in.

He leaned in the doorway, face once again tantalizingly close.

"Hey. Thanks for today, Fee. I mean it. You've gone way above and beyond. And I enjoyed hanging out with you. Do you think . . ." He bit his lip, hesitating. "You think maybe we could hang out, just for fun? Maybe at Wild Rose Days next Saturday? Just the two of us? I meant what I said the other night. I hope I didn't scare you off."

"Yes. I mean, no. No, you didn't scare me off, and yes, I'd love to hang out."

"It's a date, then? Saturday?"

"It's a date."

"See you at play practice tonight, then."

"See ya."

He closed the door of her car and waved her off. She didn't even try to hide the smile stretching across her face. Chase Coleman wanted to hang out with her. With her! And she had two boxes of historical treasures just waiting to be mined in her trunk. Today could not get any better.

Finally. Fiona finger combed her damp hair and climbed onto her bed, leaning back into the pile of pillows she'd stacked against the headboard. It had been a long day. A good day but a long one. Even after a warm shower, she wasn't quite ready to sleep. The boxes of books she'd brought home from the Coleman's attic beckoned. She'd stacked them beside her bed so they'd be easy to dig into.

Play practice had gone well tonight. At least as well as it ever did one week before opening night. A few actors were still bumbling their lines, but luckily, all the major parts were coming along nicely. The ending still bothered her, though. Something felt rushed or lacking or both. She couldn't quite put her finger on it, but it lacked the emotion she had wanted when she and Adele first began writing the play. She'd never liked how they'd ended it but still hadn't come up with a better option.

She wished she knew more about how Tehya had ended things with Jakob Jeremiah. Had she left one day without ever telling him? Had he decided to marry Gertrude before or after Tehya left? The diary never said. It told of Tehya seeing Gertrude and Jakob together and the jealousy she'd felt. It told of Tehya's tear-filled conversation with her dying mother, who begged her to leave Jakob behind. Both those scenes they'd added to the play. But then the diary entries had stopped.

What had happened to Tehya? Fiona knew there had never been a double suicide up on Wild Rose Ridge as the earlier play depicted. Chase's family was proof enough of that. Had Tehya taken her own life and that of her baby? Or had she done as her mother requested and gone to live with family on the Yakama reservation? She and Adele had suspected the second option, given the diary ended up at the library there, but there had been no entries to confirm it. Had Tehya delivered a healthy baby? Had she lived a happy life? Maybe the fact Fiona still had so many questions was why the ending she'd written felt so unsatisfying. Hopefully, the audience wouldn't feel the same way because she didn't have time to change things now.

Sighing, she reached inside the top box and pulled out a pile of ledgers. As she had noted in the attic, the top one was dated in the mid-1920s and detailed farm expenses and income for two years. Pulling one from the bottom of the stack, she quickly scanned the dates. 1895. Closer, but still not the early dates she was hoping for. She fanned through each of the ledgers in her pile, looking for papers stuck in between the pages. A few bills and receipts fell out, but nothing that looked like a land deed or map.

Charlotte, who had followed Fiona into bed, batted at one of the slips of paper as it fell. Fiona rescued it and slipped it back into the pages of the ledger. Absently rubbing Charlotte under her chin and behind her ears, Fiona glanced at her phone to check the time. Almost midnight. And yet.

"What do you think, Charlotte? Do we keep looking?"

Charlotte's purr was all the answer she needed.

Diving back into the box, she located a couple of leather-bound journals. Flipping one open, she saw the date 1886. This was more like it, except . . . it was written in German. The information they needed might be written right here, but there was no way she was going to find it until they could get it translated. Ivy could help. She'd studied German in high school and then spent six months with a baker in Munich learning pastry arts. She had a vested interest, too, considering this was her family's history also.

Peering back into the box, Fiona pulled out a few antique books and scanned the titles and front matter. An 1878 book on what looked to be botany and an early 1880s church hymnal. She set them aside to start a pile for Benedict to research their worth.

Pulling out another book, she found an antique copy of *Ben Hur*. She opened it to the flyleaf. *Jakob Jeremiah*, the script read, *his book*. She skimmed her fingers across the name. Jakob Jeremiah. Seeing his signature made him more real. Sure, she knew he had lived, but he'd lived so long in her imagination that sometimes she forgot he was real.

She flipped to the publication page and read the date. 1880. A first publication? She examined the book more closely. Leather bound, in good condition, binding in good shape. This could be worth some money. She carefully spread the book open to examine the spine. Was that a paper tucked inside there?

Throwing back her covers and dislodging Charlotte, who had settled in to sleep beside her, Fiona raced to the desk in the next room. She pulled out her box of book repair tools and rummaged around until she found her long tweezers. Gently, she spread the spine again and fished for an edge of the folded paper. She gave a tug. The paper didn't budge. Carefully, she tugged again, doing her best to apply steady pressure so the paper wouldn't tear. Yes. This time she was able to draw it out.

She dropped into her office chair and carefully unfolded the fragile paper, gasping at what she found. A letter. She recognized the script and a quick glance at the signature confirmed it. This was another letter from Tehya to Jakob Jeremiah. The date read June 7, 1886.

My dearest JJ,

Much as I struggle to write these words, I must. I am leaving. It is not what you want to hear. It is not what I want to say. But it is what must be done.

This was it. The missing piece to the puzzle. Tehya's last letter to Jakob Jeremiah. Fiona read it through. Then, she read it through again. Now she knew for sure how the story ended. She also knew how to end the play.

Chapter Seven

The backstage buzz was what Chase loved best about opening night. You could almost taste the excitement as the actors found last-minute pins for costumes and rehearsed their lines for the last time. Fiona, standing near the curtain talking to Ivy, who was the stage manager, looked especially beautiful in a simple black dress that hugged her curves in all the right places. Her long red hair hung in loose curls across her shoulders and down her back. As if sensing his stare, she turned, caught his gaze, and smiled.

He grinned back, thankful for whatever stars had aligned to make him the recipient of her smiles. He could hardly wait until tomorrow. She'd promised to spend the whole day with him. The play would continue through its six performances, but for the most part, their job as directors was done. Barring any major disasters, of course. He was looking forward to celebrating. With Fiona.

Oh sure, he'd only been at the job a few weeks, but

the added work on top of getting set up at the clinic and tracking down his family history had made life hectic. He was ready for things to slow down a bit and to have a chance to get to know Fiona better. From what he'd seen so far, she was definitely someone he wanted to be with.

Tonight she was all poise and confidence as she answered last-minute questions and put out last-minute fires. She'd made a point to say a word to each cast member. Not that he'd been watching or anything. Okay. Sure. He'd been watching her all night. In fact, he was finding it harder and harder to look away whenever she was around.

Thirty minutes ago, they had gathered the cast and crew for the opening night speech. Listening to Fiona's words of encouragement, he could tell she and this group had formed a special bond in the months leading up to this moment. He was glad he had been able to share a small part of it. He glanced at the time on his phone, then walked over to Fiona and touched her on the arm.

"Five minutes until curtain time, Madame Director. Shall we take our seats?"

She gave a tremulous smile, the first sign of nerves he'd seen all night. "I guess it's go time."

"They're going to do fine. You've prepared them well. Now it's time to sit back and enjoy."

He led her down the side stairs to their reserved seats on the front row.

"Wow." Fiona turned to him, eyes wide. "This place is packed."

Good. All his efforts over the past two weeks had

obviously paid off. The flyers, the posters, the t.v., radio, and social media ads. Who knew he had such a knack for marketing? Since the play and its directing were in capable hands, he'd pitched in where he saw a void. A packed house on opening night was a good sign. Now the play itself and word of mouth would do the rest.

The house lights dimmed. Once the room was fully dark, the curtain rose to a spotlight on Gianna Whitebird, who played Tehya. She sat in her secret cove writing in her diary. Gianna's recorded voice came across the loudspeaker.

"Today, I met the one my soul has waited for in the cove beneath the ridge where the wild roses bloom. He is beautiful, this one, and when I look into his eyes, my heart sings."

Chase sat back to enjoy the play. He'd seen all of it before, of course, in starts and spurts. He'd helped with blocking and pacing. But he'd missed the dress rehearsal because of a late appointment last night. This would be the first time he'd see it all the way through with no stops for revision or direction. Kaden Schulte, who played Jakob, stumbled a bit on his first line, his nerves coming through, but after that, he melded into character and took off. Kaden and Gianna had good chemistry onstage, and soon Chase was caught up in the story.

By the time the play reached its final scene, he was rooting for the couple to overcome all the odds stacked against them. Sure, he knew that if they had, he wouldn't be sitting here today. But this was a play. They deserved a happy ending. Fiona had told him she had changed the final scene after she found that letter in Jakob Jeremiah's book. He hadn't seen that ending yet.

In the original ending, the scene focused on Jakob and Gertrude's wedding. Tehya stood in the shadows and quietly slipped away. Now, the curtain opened to a split stage. On one side, the wedding scene was still intact, with Jakob and Gertrude standing with the preacher beneath a flowering arch. Their families all gathered around them, smiles on all their faces. On the other side was sorrow. Tehya stood by a wagon loaded with a small, black trunk. Her parents and brothers stood nearby, visibly upset. As Tehya moved to hug them each goodbye, Gianna's voice came across the loudspeaker again,

My dearest JJ,

Much as I struggle to write these words, I must. I am leaving. It is not what you want to hear. It is not what I want to say. But it is what must be done.

My parents have arranged for me to marry a man of my people, and I have agreed to go. I saw you with her today, the one your parents have chosen for you, and I knew I could not stand in her way.

She is lovely, like sunshine and lilies. You will be happy with her. I can see it.

Maybe our love would be enough in another time and place, but it will never survive this place and this time. Inevitably, it will only bring us sorrow.

You must be with your people. I must be with mine. You know this is true and right. Maybe not for ourselves, but for our children. Our love could never protect them from the hurt they will receive if we stay together.

Do not try to follow. I am steadfast in this. Following me will only cause more pain.

Stay. Be happy. Live a good life. Do this for me.

I will always remember our time together, as beautiful and pure as the wild roses on the ridge.

You have my heart always,
Your wild Indian Rose

The curtain closed, and the lights dimmed to black. Chase heard sniffling from beside him and behind. As the room lights came on and the crowd erupted in applause, he saw many women wiping their eyes. He joined the crowd on their feet as they clapped for the cast when they came to make their final bows.

He grinned at Fiona and mouthed, "You did it!" Then, at Ivy's beckoning wave, he climbed the stairs to the stage and took the microphone from her.

"I want to thank everyone for joining us tonight for the first showing of the new and improved Wild Rose Festival play. I told you it was going to be good, right? Now, I need you to spread the word so we can pack this house each and every night. We'll be here again tomorrow night and Sunday at 2 p.m. Then, we'll do it all again next weekend, so be sure to tell your friends.

"Finally, before you leave, there's someone else we need to thank for tonight's performance. Fiona, would you come up here, please."

She reddened, then walked toward the steps. As she

joined him at the microphone, Ivy came out with a large bouquet of roses he'd ordered earlier today.

Ivy handed her the flowers, and he pulled Fiona close in a side hug.

"For those who don't know, this is Fiona Jones. She and Adele Langley, who could not be here tonight, wrote this play. Then, Fiona has spent the last five months working with this group of cast members to wrestle it into what we all enjoyed tonight. Give a hand tonight, folks, to our playwright and director extraordinaire, Fiona Jones."

Once again, the crowd erupted. Chase couldn't stop grinning at the flustered beauty on her face. They'd surprised her for sure, but in a good way. Tears gathered at the corners of her eyes.

He leaned down and whispered in her ear. "Enjoy your moment. You deserve it."

~

Enjoy your moment. You deserve it.

Chase's words echoed in Fiona's thoughts as she entered the cast and crew after-party at High Ridge Cellars. Max Hanford, who played Wilhelm Kohlmann in the play, had reserved the party room for them weeks ago. Fiona had attended a wedding reception here last summer but hadn't been back since. The restaurant was far more upscale than her usual simple fare. The grounds and setting were gorgeous, of course. The rambling Mediterranean-style buildings always looked magical in the moonlight.

She could see from across the courtyard that the party was already in full swing. She, Ivy, and Jeremy had stayed behind to straighten up the auditorium and stage before the next performance. Chase had gone ahead with Max to get things settled before the cast and their guests arrived.

For not thinking she needed a co-chair for this play, she sure had come to depend on Chase and all he did. She'd tucked away one of the programs as she cleaned up tonight, amazed at the detail he'd put into their design. He'd also seen to having them all printed, along with fliers and posters he'd put up in all the businesses around town. Frankly, she wouldn't have had time to do any of that.

Enjoy your moment. You deserve it.

Did she deserve it? This perfect night? The applause? The joy of seeing it all come together after months of preparation? Maybe. She usually shied away from the term, choosing instead to consider herself blessed when good days like today happened. She stopped a minute to enjoy the view, letting Jeremy and Ivy go on ahead. The night was perfect. Chilly but not cold. A half-moon hung low in the sky over Wild Rose Lake. Ahead of her, the party room was lit up and filled with people mingling, talking, and laughing. She could see them clearly through the floor-to-ceiling windows that allowed guests an unhindered view of the lake.

Those were her people. Her crowd. She'd finally found a place where she belonged. Did she deserve it? Did anyone ever truly deserve the blessings God showered on them? No. But she was not about to let them go.

"You coming?" Ivy called from the doorway.

Breathing a prayer of gratefulness, she hurried up the stone path to join her.

Music pulsed as they stepped into the room. High and low tables were scattered throughout the room. The cast members, crew, and their families stood and sat in groups around the room. A table along the far wall was loaded with food, and wait staff circled throughout the guests offering glasses of wine and hors d'oeuvres. Fiona took red wine and a bruschetta bite from the closest server. Mmmmm. That went down way too fast.

"We need to make it to the food table, fast," she said to Ivy. "I don't think I've eaten since breakfast."

"I'm heading that way."

But before they'd gotten too far into the room, Gianna's parents stopped them.

"We wanted to tell you how much we enjoyed this new version of the play," Erin Whitebird said. "The storyline and the characters are so much more believable. I just loved it."

"Well, we loved having Gianna in the cast," Fiona replied. "She did such a wonderful job with Tehya. That girl is talented."

As Kaden's parents joined the circle, Ivy murmured in her ear. "Should I bring you a slice of pizza?"

Fiona nodded and held up two fingers as Ivy slipped off. One slice would not be nearly enough.

"So, tell us about Tehya's diary." Will Schulte jumped right in. "That was the source of the narration in the play, right? Where did you find it?"

"Adele found it. She came across it in a box of books

and papers the library at the Yakama Reservation school sent her. She brought it to me, and that's where we started with revising the play. Later, I found a stack of letters from Tehya to Jakob in Edith Coleman Richardson's estate papers. They corroborated what the diary had said."

"Really?" he glanced at his wife. "Makes you wonder what might be hiding in some of our great aunt's attics."

"You might be surprised." Fiona thought of the boxes of papers and books she still needed to go through for Chase. "Hopefully, some family treasures, at least."

Where was Chase anyway? She hadn't seen him since they'd walked in.

She finished her conversation with the Schultes and Whitebirds, then moved to the next group to thank members of the stage crew for all their hard work. Ivy came back with two slices of ham and pineapple pizza.

"Girl. You're a lifesaver." Fiona took them from her and took a big bite, savoring the combination of sweet and savory.

"We'll have to check out the dessert table later," Ivy said. "I saw some Apple Strudel and Crème Brulee."

"And you want to see how they measure up to yours."

"Of course not. I've never been able to master Crème Brulee."

"That's not true. And we all know you make the best Apple Strudel in town. All that German training has not gone to waste. I promise you." Fiona took another bite of pizza and looked around again. "Have you seen Chase?"

Ivy's expression turned vague. "I'm not sure. Maybe earlier."

Jeremy, who had taken a seat with his other stage crew members, pointed over the crowd toward the bar. "He's over there. With Portia."

Portia? The pizza suddenly grew tasteless—the night far less magical. There was only one Portia. Portia Morales. Now Fiona knew why Ivy was acting so vague.

"I didn't know she was going to be here," Fiona said to Ivy under her breath.

Ivy shrugged. "She does own the place. Or at least her family does. There's rarely a party where Portia doesn't show up. Besides, she has a cousin in the play, right?"

Oh. Right. George Morales played one of Tehya's brothers. Fiona hadn't known the two were cousins, but it made sense. Half the town was related to the Morales clan, it seemed. Fiona moved further into the room to get a better look at the crowd by the bar. Sure enough, Portia was in the middle of a group of all men. Worst of all, she was hanging on Chase's arm as if she owned him. Maybe she did. They had dated in high school, after all. Maybe tonight was a long overdue reunion.

Just then, Chase glanced up and caught Fiona looking at him. He shot her a huge grin, disentangled himself from Portia, and began walking her way. When he left, Portia gave a little pout, then turned and latched onto the next guy in the circle. So, maybe not a reunion after all. Maybe simply classic Portia.

"Hey," Chase said as he reached them. "I was wondering where you had got to. Everything go okay back at the auditorium?"

"Yes, everything's ready for tomorrow. What's that you're wearing?" She pointed to a button on his shirt with

Portia's face on it. "Portia Morales. Hometown Pride. What's that all about?"

Chase glanced down at it. "Oh, Portia's gone all political, I guess. Says she's running for city councilwoman. She's pinning them on everyone she sees."

Beside her, Ivy gasped. "You've got to be kidding!"

"I don't think so. Why?"

"Fiona's running for that council seat. Has been since Ellen Sutherland stepped down for health reasons in March."

"For real? Why didn't I know about this?"

"Because, as of yesterday, I was running unopposed," Fiona said. The deadline for filing was today. "I guess Portia decided to put her hat in the ring." Which meant Fiona might as well kiss that dream goodbye. She didn't stand a ghost of a chance going against a hometown girl. Never had.

Chase unpinned the button from his shirt and set it on the table behind them. "Guess I won't be needing that, then. You'll need to give me one of yours to put in its place."

"That's just it. I don't have one. I've been so busy with the play that I didn't even think to print up campaign stuff. I thought I'd be running unopposed and had plenty of time. Guess I didn't think that through very well."

Why was she tearing up over this? How embarrassing. Chase would think she was lame to get so upset about a silly election. Only, it hadn't been silly to her. She loved this small town and had hoped she'd finally found her place. Giving back as a councilwoman was a way of proving she belonged here. That she was finally part of a community that knew her name and counted her as one of their own.

But no one was going to vote for her over the ever-bubbly Portia Morales. The girl who was voted Most Popular in high school. The one whose father owned the most prosperous winery in the area. The one who was the life of every party and drop-dead gorgeous to boot. Fiona didn't stand a chance.

Fiona cleared her throat and pasted on a smile. "Hey, tonight isn't about elections. Tonight, we have a play to celebrate, right? I say we go raid the dessert table."

Fiona had rented one of the booths on the sidewalk down by the lake this year to give Rosehips Tea and Books exposure in two locations. Those trolling Main Street would see a display with samples outside her shop's door. Those who stuck to the beach area would see this one. She'd been sure to include fliers for the play in both locations and a card advertising her podcast. What she didn't have was promotional material for her campaign for the city council.

How could she have been so naive as to think she wouldn't need that yet? She looked toward the High Ridge Cellars booth where Portia had set up shop this morning. She'd decorated a small table beside their main booth in red, white, and blue ribbons. An arch above the table read: Hometown Roots; Hometown Pride. A large yard sign beside the table featured Portia's picture and the words Vote Portia, City Council. As local people strolled by, Portia was quick to greet them and hand them a campaign button and a wine bottle stopper with her face and logo on it.

Ivy had just now dropped one in front of Fiona when she brought her a blueberry cream cheese Danish on her break from the Weaver Bakery booth just down the line. Maybe the Danish was supposed to soften the blow, but all the sugar in the world wasn't going to hide the fact that Fiona had botched this campaign badly.

"How long do you think Portia has been planning this?" she asked Ivy.

Ivy shrugged. "You never know with Portia. A few weeks at least to have ordered all the promo stuff."

"So why would she have waited until the last day to file her bid for the election?"

"I'm guessing it was to catch you off guard."

"Well, it worked. Though, I really should have thought about today being a good chance to get the word out that I was running. I was so tied up with the play that I didn't even think about it. Other than the ad I've been running on the podcast each week, I haven't done much at all."

"Who would have thought you would need to? The last three candidates for city council ran unopposed. It's pretty much a theme here in Wild Rose Ridge. No one really wants the job, so the same four people run term after term. Honestly, I can't remember a time when Ellen Sutherland wasn't on the council. She'd probably still be there if she hadn't gotten so sick. Arlan taking out old Mr. Schulte for mayor was the last time we've had a turnover of any kind." Ivy turned from watching Portia to look at

Fiona's booth. "Your booth looks great, by the way. I'm glad you decided to join us here on the beach this year."

"I'm hoping we'll get a little more traffic when the games pick up this afternoon." The town had scheduled a beach volleyball tournament for today, followed by a cornhole competition. Both events were sure to draw crowds.

"Where's Chase? I thought you were supposed to spend the day with him."

"Something came up at the clinic this morning. He said he'd try to get here by noon. It's probably for the best since I was the only one available to man this booth this morning. Benedict and Katie Rose are handling the shop. Jeremy and Colton said they'd watch the booth this afternoon."

"You're going to trust those two techie geeks with your booth all afternoon?"

"They've proved pretty reliable on the stage crew so far. Invaluable even. Besides, there's not much to do here other than give out tea samples and take money from anyone who wants to buy one of the bargain books. Most of the heavy labor is taking place back at the shop."

"Oh," Ivy's face lit up. "I almost forgot. We have our first review on the play." She pulled a newspaper out of her bag and handed it to Fiona.

Fiona took it a little reluctantly. "Please tell me it's not by Marla Mavis."

"Well, it is. But it's not what you think. She's much nicer this year."

Fiona scanned the headline. Annual Festival Play Surprises. Hmmm. Surprise good, or surprise bad?

The cast of Where the Wild Roses Bloom *provided us with a treat last night when they performed the new and improved version of the annual Wild Rose Festival play. Gone were the hackneyed phrases and predictable plot of the original play. In its place was a poignant tale of love and loss that had the power to affect this audience member deeply. Fiona Jones and Adele Langley have crafted a haunting story of weight and beauty.*

"Wow. She *was* nice. 'Weight and beauty.' I like that."

"Kinda makes up for the Portia thing, right?"

Fiona grinned at her friend. "Almost."

"Then my work here is done. I need to get back and help Mom." With a quick side hug, Ivy headed up the sidewalk, turning after she'd gone a few steps. "I almost forgot," she said as she continued walking backward. "Remind me to tell you what I found in that journal you gave me."

"What did you find?"

"I'll tell you later."

Fiona would have chased after her if she hadn't heard the words, "Excuse me."

Two thirty-something moms with their pre-school-aged girls had stopped in front of the booth. "Are you giving samples of your teas?"

"Yes, of course. What would you like to try? We have The Lizzy named after Elizabeth Bennet. And this one, my personal favorite, is the Anne Shirley from *Anne of Green Gables*. Our third sample is The Huckleberry Finn. A friend of mine inspired the ingredients of that one. You'll find all the flavors listed there on the cards. Would you like to try one, or maybe one of each?"

After she had served both ladies and their little girls and pointed them toward her shop, the foot traffic picked up. The morning passed quickly as she talked tea and books with all kinds of people. This is what she loved most about Wild Rose Ridge. The people. Both locals and visitors. There was never a dull moment, especially from the Spring Festival season right up until the fall. She'd sent another group off toward Main Street and Rosehips when Jeremy, Colton, and Chase arrived, each carrying a box.

"What's all this?"

"I'll show you in a minute," Chase said. "I just need to grab a few more things."

A few minutes later, he was back, a card table under one arm and a large sign under the other. As he turned the sign around, Fiona noticed it was a campaign sign with her headshot on it. *Time for Change with Fiona*, the slogan read. Fiona for City Council was written in smaller letters beneath it.

The boys began unpacking the boxes as Chase set up the table and placed a red tablecloth over it. From the first one, they pulled out stacks of fliers, bookmarks, notepads, and buttons. All sported the same slogan. The next box held white ball caps, and the last had white t-shirts with her name and slogan in red and blue. He threw each of the boys a t-shirt, then pulled one on over his shirt.

"Here," he said. "Grab one in your size and put it on. I hear they are all the rage this season."

"Chase, how in the world did you do all this in one morning?"

"Well, to be perfectly honest, I started some of it last

night. Besides, I'd had a trial run with most of the printers in town with all the promotional material for the play. Let's just say I know people. Portia isn't the only one with a hometown advantage. Now, the bookmarks should pair well with your brand. I also found a place that will personalize tea bags, but they won't be done until Monday. Should still give you time to hand them out to the crowds this week."

"This is . . . you are . . ."

"Amazing? Fantastic? Spectacular?"

"Wonderful." She threw her arms around him, and he pulled her into a warm hug. "Honestly, I can't thank you enough."

"I'm happy to be of service. Now." He kept one arm around her shoulders while he grabbed a t-shirt from the box with his other hand. "Let's get you into uniform. We'll leave the boys here to man the booth while we campaign. Oh, and if you see any willing Fiona sponsors in the crowd, be sure they get them a t-shirt and a hat also."

Fiona pulled one of the t-shirts on over her tank top and pulled her braid up and through the hole in the back of the ball cap.

"Ready," she said.

"Good." He took her hand. "Let's go greet your voters, Miss Jones."

He led her up the sidewalk past the High Ridge Cellars booth, where Portia stood staring with a decidedly sour look on her face. As they passed Weaver's Bakery booth, she noticed Mrs. Weaver and Ivy wearing her t-shirts. In the next booth, Rose Stevens of Rose's

Dance and Yoga Studio also had one on. They all waved as Chase and Fiona walked by.

Fiona couldn't contain her smile. She loved this town. She was also developing a decided fondness for the handsome doctor who had made all this possible. A part of her cautioned that she was falling way too soon and way too fast, but at the moment, the rest of her just didn't care.

Chapter Eight

The sun was shining its first rays above the Beaverhead Bluffs when Chase drove through town toward Rose Cove. Shoot thinning day. He hadn't spent nearly as much time at the vineyard as he had hoped since coming home. But he'd promised Dad he'd help today and didn't want to disappoint. Getting started in the new practice and helping with the play had put a huge dent in his time. But he'd taken today off and planned to make up for the lost time.

The last time he'd been home, he and Fiona had searched the attic. He couldn't help smiling when he thought of her. Saturday had been a great day. They'd spent the afternoon participating in the cornhole tournament and eating way too much at the booths and food trucks that lined the lakefront. Fiona wasn't the most skilled partner in cornhole, but she was sure fun to watch. Her energy and genuine interest in people made her almost irresistible. He could tell the townspeople liked her. She might not think it, but she had a good chance of besting Portia in this election.

Portia. She sure hadn't changed much. Manipulating events, so they played only in her favor. Waiting until the last minute to announce her participation in an election to catch her competition off guard was classic Portia behavior. Thank goodness he'd been able to help Fiona jump-start her campaign and narrow any advantage Portia might have had. Nope. Much as he'd like to say he'd forgiven Portia for all those old wounds, obviously, he hadn't.

He pulled into the drive at Rose Cove, steering his truck toward the barns and outbuildings rather than the house today. Dad was talking to two young people Chase didn't recognize over by the first row of Rieslings. Probably the interns. Chase hadn't met them yet but knew they were supposed to be here by now.

Pete Sandina, Dad's foreman, called a greeting as Chase climbed out of his truck. Dad had told him several of Pete's family would be here this week to help with the thinning. From the looks of the rows he could see close to the barn, they'd made good progress yesterday.

He wished he could help more than just today, knowing the acres of vines that still needed thinning, but the rest of his week was booked. Grapes had to be one of the most labor-intensive crops he knew. It was always an all-hands-on-deck approach throughout the growing and harvest seasons. He could remember many late spring days, coming home from school and being sent out to thin the vines.

Dad walked over and gave his shoulder a soft punch. "Thanks for coming."

"No problem."

Dad motioned to the two people beside him. "I don't think you've met Levi and Brook yet. They're both taking viticulture at WSU in Wenatchee. They'll be helping out this summer. This is my son, Chase."

Chase shook hands with the interns, then turned back to Dad.

"I'm ready to get going. Where do you want me to start?"

"We started at the barn yesterday and have been working our way out. Just look for the first row to the north that's not thinned and go from there."

"Will do."

"You remember what you're doing?"

Chase grinned. "I'm pretty sure I could do it in my sleep. Fist width apart?"

"Yup."

"See ya at lunch."

Chase walked along the rows of vines admiring the way the early morning sun lit the branches. He spied Pete's wife, Rosie, already a third of the way down one row. Their son, Trey, worked the next one. Waving a greeting, he headed to the empty row next to Trey.

He examined the vine in front of him. Vine growth had been vigorous in the last three weeks, which meant plenty of these shoots had to go. Chase started in, keeping only the healthiest shoots and trying to create enough spacing to ensure plenty of airflow. Grandpa Ben had always told them to keep a fist-sized width between the shoots. Of course, when they were young, sometimes two fists worked better.

Some of the vineyards in the area were experimenting with automated ways to thin and prune, but Chase liked this hands-on approach. It made him feel more connected to the growing process. He wondered how many people knew the amount of labor that went into each glass of wine they consumed. He knew he never took a sip without thinking about all the pruning, thinning, and suckering that went into producing all those grapes. And then there was the wine-making process itself. That area was Greek to him. But the grape-growing part he knew.

He was nowhere near ready to hang up his stethoscope, but he did enjoy days like this where he could get out in the fresh air, leave the smells and urgency of the clinic behind, and work hands-on with the crop. The work was repetitive, sure, but it gave a person plenty of time to think. There was something elementally satisfying about planting something and watching it grow. Kind of like working in partnership with the Creator to bring forth life from the ground.

As he worked, his mind drifted from one topic to another, finally settling on the vineyard itself. He loved the fact that in working this land today, he was essentially carrying on a family tradition that started five generations ago. But what was the future of this land? Would his generation be the one who let it go? He knew Dad was still pinning his hopes on Oliver, but he needed to let that dream die. Oliver had no interest in small-town living.

The last time Chase had visited Oliver in Los Angeles, the man couldn't stay off his phone for more than five minutes at a time. Chase had thought emergency room work in Seattle was demanding until he'd watched Oliver chase high-end real estate deals in LA. The difference was, unlike himself, Oliver loved that kind of adrenaline. Chase couldn't imagine his brother ever settling for the slower life of a farmer.

And Tori? She was all about travel and photography right now. Maybe someday she'd want to come home, but he didn't see it happening any time soon. He was the only one of the three who wanted a life here in Wild Rose Ridge, but his heart was in medicine, not agriculture. Much as he loved coming out and spending days like this in the vineyard, he didn't want to manage a winery full-time.

And then there was Dad with his dreams of making this place as successful as their neighbors at High Ridge Cellars. Like that was going to happen. The Morales family had been in the wine-making business for more than twenty years. Dad was barely eight years in. Even if their family did own the vines that had skyrocketed High Ridge Cellars into a winery of world-renowned fame, that didn't mean Dad would be able to replicate the wine. Not unless he could find someone like Ashton Morales, the enologist over at High Ridge who was a wizard at coaxing new flavors out of the grapes. That type of vintnery took years of training and a whole lot of talent. As far as he knew, Dad had none of that.

Which made him wonder why his father was so set on finding that old deed. From what Ivy had told him and

Fiona on Saturday, Wilhelm Kohlmann's journal confirmed Tehya's diary. Wilhelm and Jacques had indeed planted a vineyard from the Lemberger vines on both sides of the property line. Who was to say that the ones on the Morales property were not the only ones to survive?

It wasn't like his family had given much care to that vineyard back when this place used to be an apple orchard. Grandpa Ben and his father were teetotalers, and though Grandpa had decided to grow grapes like many others in this valley back when the apple harvest tanked in the seventies, he would only sell his grapes to the jelly companies for the first two decades. He only agreed to sell to a winery when his good friend René Bouchard, Ashton's grandfather, approached him about it when the family had decided to go into the winery business. So why the fuss about the deed?

The question was still niggling at him as he and Dad walked through the barrel storage room in the basement of the new building Dad had built when he decided to try his hand at winemaking. He gave Chase a taste of the wine he'd entered in the Washington Winegrowers Association's contest that would be awarded in July. It was a good wine, but Chase didn't know if it was an award-winning wine. But then, Chase was no connoisseur.

"You doing all right, Dad?" Once again, Chase was struck by how tired Dad was looking. "Have you given any more thought to coming in for a physical? I could schedule you for next week."

"You know I don't have time for that this time of year. I'm fine. Stop trying to doctor me. So, did you and Fiona have any luck in your attic search the other day? Your mother said you found a few treasures."

"Yeah. But not the deed yet." He looked over at Dad, pondering whether to stir things up. "I was pretty young when this whole controversy with the Morales family started. Remind me again why we need the deed. From what Fiona found in great aunt Edith's attic and what Ivy translated out of Wilhelm Kohlmann's journal, it seems that those vines could legitimately belong to High Ridge. Both sources show that Wilhelm had shared some of the family vines with them."

"Some of the vines, maybe. But not all of them. And certainly, not all the land they claim is theirs. Something is fishy about the deed recorded at the county auditor's office. It's the one Franco Morales claims belonged to the Bouchard family. You know our cove?"

"Rose Cove. Yes." *Beneath the ridge where the wild roses grow.* He wouldn't be able to think of it any other way from now on. "What about it?"

"Back in my father's day, even back in my childhood in the seventies, we knew our property line extended at least two acres beyond the northern edge of the cove. Now the line is only a quarter acre from that point, at the most. The dispute started shortly after Franco took over High Ridge after Ashton's mom and dad died back in ninety-five. Franco claimed the vines planted in that section belonged to him, and he had a deed to prove it."

"Wouldn't there have been a deed already on file for both properties? They've been in our family and theirs for over a hundred years."

"That's the problem. The original deeds were filed at

the land office in Waterville, which burned down in 1897. If you wanted to prove ownership of one of the homesteads recorded before 1897, you had to show a copy of your deed, which the government sent once a landowner proved a homestead. I guess our family never bothered to send one because there isn't one on file. By the time the land came into dispute, we couldn't find our original deed. We had nothing to back our claim other than how we had farmed it the past hundred years, and no one in the Bouchard family was left who could corroborate those facts. We had to concede that land to Franco."

"Well. There were a few boxes left in the attic that we didn't have time to check last time. I'll go through them before I leave today to see if anything shows up."

"Sounds great. I appreciate your help, Chase. It means a lot to see you back here working the vines. Now, if we could get your brother back here for a visit, between the two of us, we might be able to convince him to stay. His business savvy is just what we need. Did I tell you he made another multi-million-dollar deal? That boy sure has the knack for success."

Would there ever be a conversation with Dad where he didn't bring up Oliver? Maybe someday he would realize Oliver wasn't the golden boy he'd always thought he was, the one destined to save Rose Cove. But it would sure be nice, just once, to hear his dad brag like that about him.

∽

After a dinner of his mom's specialty lasagna, Chase climbed the steps to the attic and headed to the far section where they'd found the door in the knee wall. He crawled into the narrow space, remembering how it had felt with Fiona tucked in beside him. He'd really wanted to kiss her that day, but after her reaction to his first kiss, he'd been afraid he'd scare her off for good. Besides, he knew better than to rush into things with a girl. He'd learned to be cautious after Portia.

Chase searched a few more boxes finding only old dishes and table linens. Flashing the light on his phone into the far corner, he spotted one more small trunk. He pulled it toward him and lifted the lid. This looked promising. The box was filled with papers, file folders, and a few picture frames. He leafed through an accordion-style folder to see copies of old farm receipts. He dug further into the box, drawing out a very old-looking leather pouch.

Opening it, he pulled out a yellowed piece of parchment paper that had been folded in quarters. He unfolded it to find what looked like a hand-drawn map. He shined his light on the heading at the top to read the words: Rose Cove Farm established 1886. Not a legal deed, but this could be a big help. If this was drawn in the early days of the homestead, it should show landmarks and other details that could help them find the original boundaries. He set it aside to look at later in a better light.

Turning back to the trunk, he pulled out three picture frames. Two were pictures of people, as he'd expected, but one was a framed certificate of some kind.

Again, with the help of his flashlight, he was able to read the large heading. Homestead. Land Office at Waterville, Washington. March 15, 1886. He read the words again, hardly believing what he was seeing. This was it. This was the deed. At some point in time, his ancestors had framed it. Maybe they even hung it in a place of prominence on some wall in this very house, but it had since been tucked away and forgotten as if the significance of such a document was of no value at all. Grabbing the three frames and the pouch, he backed out of the tiny crawl space and into the better light of the attic. *Wilhelm Kohlmann*, the deed read, *has made payment in full for . . .* The coordinates and ordinal directions made little sense to him, but a register of deeds could tell him what they meant. They could also tell him if they corroborated the property description given by the Morales family.

This was golden. At last, they could determine which family had the right to that northwest section and put this argument to rest once and for all. He pulled out the hand-drawn map again and looked at it more closely. He was amazed at the amount of detail the artist had put into it. Like the journal Fiona had found, the key to the map had been written in German. He'd need Ivy's help again to know the scale of the map for sure, but from looking at the controversial northwest corner of the map, he could see the distance between the cove and the boundary was a lot more than half an acre.

This was huge. He was tempted to run downstairs and share what he'd found with Dad and Mom, but something held him back. What if this proved what the

Morales family claimed instead of the other way around? Dad would be devastated. No. He'd keep this to himself until he had proof one way or another. There were landmarks on this map that could still be there. The way the ridge curved at the boundary line. A stand of trees was drawn along the border and a stone wall, like Tehya's diary had said. Maybe he could find some physical evidence to prove the border was where his family said it was. Some old stones or tree roots. Something might still be there. If it weren't already so dark, he'd go out there tonight.

He worked all day tomorrow, but he had Thursday morning off. Adrenaline coursed through him. He had to share this with someone. No way he could just head home and go to bed.

He pulled out his phone and sent a text to Fiona.

Want to do some exploring Thursday morning? I found a map.

A response came back almost immediately. *What!? Of your family's vineyard?*

Yes. And the deed.

Chase! That's wonderful! The actual deed? Does it prove what you thought it would?

I can't tell yet, but it's a start. Will you be up for a while? I can bring it over.

Yes. Absolutely! And yes to the exploring as well. I'm so excited for you!

See you in a bit.

Chase folded the map and placed it carefully in the pouch. Glancing at the two framed photos in his pile, he smiled. Fiona was going to want to see these too. In fact, he couldn't wait to see her face when he showed her the photo of the original Kohlmann family and the picture of Jakob and Gertrude on their wedding day.

Chapter Nine

"You haven't told your dad about this map yet?" Fiona followed Chase across a small pasture and toward another section of vines planted against the ridge at the northwest section of the Coleman property.

"I don't want to get his hopes up in case this doesn't prove anything. He's got enough on his plate right now with the growing season and a shortage of workers. If we find something today, and I get some answers from Hardin at the county auditor's office soon, then I'll let him know."

Chase stopped and held up the map. "Okay. Look here. We have a pretty clear view of the cove and the ridge from here."

Fiona followed his gaze to where Wild Rose Ridge rose high above the vineyards. Hard to believe it had been almost three weeks since she fell down the incline on the other side of that ridge. Other than the moments when her scar would itch, she hardly thought about the accident anymore. How could it be only three weeks since Chase re-entered her life? Having seen him almost every day since then, she could barely remember a time when he wasn't an integral part of her days. Working together with him on the play contributed to most of that. Now the festival was winding down, would she see him as much? She hoped so. The fact he'd asked her to help him today had to mean something, didn't it? Or was she still thirteen-year-old Fiona seeing possibilities where there were none?

"There," Chase said, drawing her thoughts back to the task at hand. "You can see the north edge of the cove right there." He pointed. "And here it is on the map. Now, what did Ivy say the distance key was?"

"One inch equals one hectare."

"What the heck is a hectare? Is that a German measurement?"

"European, I think. Here. It's in her text. A hectare equals about two and a half acres."

"Okay. Now we're getting somewhere. On this map, Wilhelm wrote that the distance between the edge of the cove and the far edge of our property was one hectare. That would be about the distance of two and a half football fields. Look at that gravel pathway that separates our property from High Ridge. Does that look like it sits two and a half football fields away from the cove?"

Fiona shook her head. "Not even half a football field."

"Exactly. The land they claim is their property starts a quarter acre from the cove, but my Grandpa Ben and my dad believe that section has always been the site of our old family vineyard. The one Wilhelm talks about in his journal. Back when I was a kid, my Grandma Martha used to make jelly out of those grapes. You can see it right here on the map. Right where their property supposedly starts. What does it say there?"

"Die Lemberger Weinstock."

"I don't need Ivy to translate that. That means Lemberger vines. The ones Wilhelm brought from Germany. And he planted them there. On our property. Not theirs."

"But he did share with the Bouchards. We have proof of that from two first-hand sources."

"We also have proof that there was once a wall built along the property line. And a strand of trees. That comes from those first-hand sources as well. And you can see them drawn here on the map."

"So, what are you hoping to find?"

"Evidence. Either wall fragments or tree roots or both. I think our best bet is up next to the ridge because that's where the trees grew. Plus, the ground there has never been planted, so the rocks and roots would not have been tilled up over the years."

"Let's do it. Where should we start?"

"I guess, to keep it fair, we'll start where the Morales family says the property line is. If we don't find anything, we'll measure off a hectare from the edge of the cove and look there."

"You have something that measures hectares? I thought you didn't even know what they were." Fiona couldn't help teasing him a little.

He gave her a playful push. "No. But I do have this map. Look at the ridge line. See how it dips here? And there's this valley that flows right along here. Now, look at the ridge. See, there's the dip. And there's the valley. The lot line should be right about there. Thank goodness, great, great, great, great Grandpa Wilhelm was a good artist."

He really was. The map had almost photographic detail to it. "Did you inherit these artistic genes?"

"Not me. That would be all Tori."

Oh, right. His world-traveling sister, who was now somewhere in France. Why was it people always wanted what they didn't have? Tori had never wanted to stay put, while Fiona would kill for roots like Tori's and Chase's that went five generations deep. Fiona had spent at least five years of her childhood living in seven different houses in three different countries on two continents. She didn't know the meaning of the word roots, but she was sure trying to grow some now.

She and Chase didn't spend much time looking in the area High Ridge claimed to be the property line. When they got there, they found a deep gully that clearly had been there for some time. There was no sign of a wall or trees anywhere near that location. Chase located the gully on the map and began walking north from there until they reached a spot that matched the terrain of the property line on the map.

Fiona looked back toward the edge of the cove. Yep. She could picture a couple of football fields between here and there. There was a patch of dogwoods growing between the vines and the bottom of the ridge at this location. Chase dropped to all fours and started examining the ground underneath them. Fiona dropped down beside him.

"What are you looking for?"

"Tree stumps. Check in the grass behind these bushes. If there was a row of trees growing here, they might have cut them off ground level rather than pulling them up. I'm guessing trees that old would have had some pretty wide trunks." Chase stood up and picked up the shovel he'd brought with him. "I'm going to start digging a few holes to see if I come across any rocks."

Fiona glanced down the hillside toward the buildings of High Ridge Cellars off in the distance.

"What if someone sees you?"

"They won't. Their crew is working the vines on the lower slopes right now like our crew is. And you can't see this section from the Morales's house. Besides, if anyone asks, I'll tell them I'm looking for a time capsule I buried up here when I was a kid."

"You did?"

"Nope. But they don't know that."

She shook her head at him. Honestly.

Starting in the tall grass behind the bushes, she pushed aside the overgrown weeds to look at the ground. A few yards up, she found a large tree trunk cut level with the ground, then another.

"Chase, I think I found something."

She'd found three trunks in a row, each a few feet apart by the time Chase came over.

"This is it," Chase said. "Here's another over here. Good eye, Jones." He took another look at the map. "Now, if the tree line was here, the wall would have started right about here, I think."

He sunk his shovel into the ground and started to work.

"We should have brought two shovels. I could have helped." As she walked toward him, she tripped over a rise in the dirt. "Umm. Doc? You might want to bring that shovel over here."

"Did you find something?"

"I'd say so."

Chase walked over and gave a whistle. The tops of what looked like a solid row of rocks peaked just above the ground's surface.

"That's the wall. I'd bet my life on it." Chase started digging in earnest, soon uncovering several layers of rocks stacked on top of each other, all in a straight line. No way those had fallen like that naturally. Someone had stacked them that way. Chase let out a whoop and picked Fiona up in a bear hug, swinging her around.

"We found it. *You* found it! This is it. This is the property line."

When Chase set her down again, Fiona looked back over the rows and rows of vines that ran between this point and the gravel path that marked what was supposed to be the edge of Coleman property. All of these rows of healthy Lemberger vines should belong to the Colemans, not the Morales family.

This was huge.

"Now what?" she asked. "Are you going to show your dad?"

"Not yet. I want to see what Hardin has to say about

the deeds first. See if he knows a reason why there would be a discrepancy. But the fact that we found the wall, the one that Jacques Bouchard himself built to divide his property from ours, is monumental. This could change everything."

As they walked back through the vineyards toward the house and barn, Chase took her hand, threading his fingers through hers. Such a small gesture, but Fiona could feel the connection all the way to her toes. Did he feel it too?

"Thanks for helping me today, Fiona. If it weren't for your sharp eyes, I might never have found any of that."

"And don't forget my clumsiness. Tripping over the rock wall counts for something."

He laughed. "You know, we've both worked pretty hard the last few weeks. I think it's time we took some time off to celebrate. How'd you like to sail out to the island with me on Sunday afternoon? We'll be all done with our commitment to the play by then. We could explore the caves. Do a little fishing. I haven't been over there since I got back. What do you think?"

"Are you finally making good on that rain check?"

"What?"

He didn't remember. Of course, he didn't. Their sailing date that never happened was more than a decade ago. She knew that day had always meant way more to her than it ever did to him. The question was, was she ready to risk her heart on him again?

"What do you mean by rain check?"

She shook her head. "Never mind. It's nothing. I'd love to come sailing with you. What can I bring?"

"Not a thing. Other than yourself. I'll take care of the rest."

Was she foolish to let herself get so excited about another chance of a sailing date with Chase? She could tell herself to guard her heart all day long, but she had a sinking feeling it was far too late.

Chase checked the rigging on the Sun Cat one more time, then glanced up the sidewalk toward Main Street for what had to be the twentieth time. Man, he had it bad. He'd talked to Fiona a couple of hours ago after church when they made their plans to meet. Yet, he could hardly wait for her to get here so he could be with her again.

They'd seen each other practically every day since he found her limping down High Ridge Road on her injured leg. But their time together never seemed like enough. When he wasn't with her, he was thinking about the next time he could be with her. He hadn't fallen for a girl this fast since Portia. And that scared him. He'd learned his lesson then, or so he'd thought. *Don't go all in too soon.* Or, in his case, *don't go all in at all.* The few relationships he'd had since Portia had been casual—surface-level at best. He'd had no trouble moving on when they were over.

But he wasn't so sure he could do that with Fiona. He wasn't even sure he wanted to. Yet, they'd known each other only three weeks. He glanced toward Main once again and finally saw her strolling around the corner headed his way. She didn't see him yet, so he took the opportunity to admire those long, tanned legs and that bright, red ponytail swinging behind her, showing glints of gold in the sunlight. She was equal parts girl next door and way out of his league, and he was hooked.

He called her name and waved as she got closer to the marina.

She smiled when she saw him and walked on down the slip toward the boat. A large beach bag hung from her shoulder. In her other hand, she carried a fishing pole. A fishing pole! If he hadn't warned himself to take things slow, he'd have kissed her right then and there.

"You brought your own pole."

"You did say something about fishing, right? Are you thinking of trying out Monster's Hole?"

"Now, how would you know about Monster's Hole?" The spot off the Monster's Cave beach on the island's west side was a popular spot for local fishermen, but a well-kept secret from outsiders.

"It was one of Pop Pop's favorites. He took me there a lot those summers I spent here."

"Sure. I remember now. I saw you out with him a couple of times. Whatever happened to his boat? A Santa Cruz 27, right? That was a beauty."

"Yeah. Pop Pop loved Old Red. I still have it. It passed down to me with the lake house. It's in storage, though. I can't bear to sell it, but it needs some work, and, honestly, I haven't had time to do much with it since I opened the bookstore."

"I could help you with that." Did he sound too eager? "Only if you wanted, of course. No pressure or anything." Boy, he was bungling this badly. "I don't know about you, but I've been itching to get back out on this lake. It was always my favorite place as a kid."

She smiled. "I remember. I loved it too." She looked down at the boat and back at him. "So, what are we waiting for, Skipper? Let's get out there."

He took her bag and rod, stored them under the seat, and then helped her aboard.

She looked around. "This isn't the same sailboat you had back in high school, is it?"

"No. Dad sold that after Oliver and I went to college. We didn't get back much in the summers after that, and Tori never did much sailing. This boat is Jason's. It's a lot like our old one, though."

She helped him cast off the lines and set the sail. He soon had the little boat tracking across the cobalt blue waters of the lake toward the island.

"You're a great first mate. We should have sailed together back when you spent your summers here. I was always out on the water. I wonder why we didn't?"

She shot him a dark look.

"What? What did I say?" Had he missed something?

"You don't remember, do you?"

"Remember what?"

"The time you kicked me off your boat to make room for Portia and her friends?"

"Wait. I kicked you off? No way."

"Absolutely. You'd asked me to come fishing with you. Just like today. Said I could be your 'first mate.' Then Portia and the other cheerleaders showed up, and you kicked me off because they needed a ride to the island, and there wasn't enough room for all of us. You said you'd give me a rain check. Seems like thirteen years is an awfully long time to make good on a 'rain check.'"

So that's what she meant the other day out at Rose Cove. He'd thought he had heard her right. Her tone was teasing, but he could tell the memory still rankled.

"Hey, I'm sorry. That was a bonehead thing to do. All I can say is that sixteen-year-old me was a jerk. *I* didn't even like the guy. Twenty-eight-year-old me is a much nicer version."

"Chase 2.0?"

"Oh, at least 5 or 6.0. There have been many glitches that have needed fixing over the years."

"I don't know. I liked sixteen-year-old Chase just fine."

"Until he kicked you off his boat."

She laughed. "Even after that. I'm the forgiving sort."

"That's good news for me. And if it makes you feel any better, if I could go back and do that day again, I'd choose you over Portia. A hundred percent."

"Why, thank you. Now, if I could convince the fine citizens of Wild Rose Ridge to do the same."

"You will. I have total faith that you will win this race for city council. Our townspeople would have to be blind not to see how much you care for them and the future of this place. We'll convince them. You'll see." He shifted the tiller to the right, pointing the small sailboat straight toward the island. "But enough of that. Today is all about rest and relaxation."

"Sounds good to me. Let's go catch some fish. You think the kokanee will still be biting?"

"I'm hoping. It may be a little late in the day for them, but I'm willing to try. Shall we try Monster's Hole first?"

"Let's do it!"

Three hours later, Chase leaned back against one of the boulders on Monster Cave Beach and watched Fiona search for monster toes along the rocky shore. Monster toes were bits of obsidian rock that could sometimes be found on this beach. They got their name, like the beach and the fishing hole, from the famous monster who supposedly lived in Wild Rose Lake. Chase and his siblings and cousins had loved looking for them as kids.

Judging just by their success at fishing, today was probably one of his worst fishing days ever. He had a gut feeling, though, it would rank as one of his favorite fishing days of all time. They'd caught only one keeper between the two of them—a nice-sized kokanee. The credit for that went entirely to Fiona. He'd caught nothing but a few small lake trout. But he couldn't remember having more fun with any other fishing partner. Fiona had made this day special.

He watched her now as she slowly strolled the shoreline, hair aglow in the late afternoon sun. Hers was more than an outward beauty. She was kind, smart, and fun to be with. She knew her way around a sailboat and a fishing rod too. She looked up and caught him staring. Maybe she sensed his eyes on her.

"Food ready?" She called.

"Yup."

"You should have called me," she said as she walked his way.

"Didn't want to spoil your fun. Did you find any?"

"No. I never do. Only that one the first day Pop Pop brought me to this beach. It must have been beginner's luck. So what's for lunch?"

He'd sent her off to search for monster toes while he set up their meal. He'd wanted it to be a surprise. While she was gone, he'd spread a cloth across one of the more level boulders and set out the food—sandwiches and bakery items he'd picked up at his aunt's bakery after church.

"Ooh. Vi's chicken salad. My favorite. How did you know?"

He didn't. But Ivy did, he was guessing. She was the one who packed the basket for them. But he did know this. He pulled out a jug of the Anne Shirley iced tea he'd asked Katie Rose to make up for him yesterday.

"Tea?" She glanced at the label. "You remembered!"

"Only the best for my favorite redhead."

She laughed. "You should have brought along a Rose Cove wine."

"I'm saving that for sunset."

"Thanks for taking care of all this, Chase. It looks delicious. Next time I'll make all the arrangements. Deal?"

"If it means there will be a next time, then absolutely."

"It's been a fun day, right? See what you missed by not bringing me with you thirteen years ago?"

"If I remember correctly, I spent that whole day following Portia and her BFF's around, holding all their gear while some photographer took pictures of them. I hadn't realized that all she wanted from me was to be her chauffeur and gopher, or I would have definitely taken you."

"I thought you and Portia started dating after that."

"I thought so too, but looking back, I'm not sure she ever considered us boyfriend and girlfriend."

"What do you mean?"

Shoot. Was he really going to go there? Share the most humiliating time of his life with the one girl he wanted most to impress? But something inside him prompted him to be honest. For some reason, he wanted her to know how foolish he had been. He wanted to share everything with her.

"What I mean is my relationship with Portia was pretty one-sided. But I didn't know it back then." He'd been mighty full of himself that summer and early fall. Oliver had decided to stay and work in Los Angeles after his first year at UCLA, so Chase had been out from under his shadow for almost a year. He was finally bulking up and finding his footing athletically. He'd made the varsity football team. He wasn't nearly the athlete Oliver had been in high school, but he wasn't bad. And Dad was starting to notice. He came to all his games and cheered him on. Top that with the fact that the head cheerleader wanted to hang out with him. Well, he wasn't surprised he'd been such a jerk to Fiona back then. He'd pretty much been a jerk to everyone. Way too big for his britches. Until that Thanksgiving.

"Aunt Violet used to host these big family gatherings every Thanksgiving. Maybe Ivy's mentioned them? By the time I was in high school, we would invite our closest friends to join us. Between Oliver and me,

Arlan and Jason, not to mention Ivy and Tori, we'd have quite a few of our classmates there. It became the party to be at over the Thanksgiving holiday. In addition to the huge meal, we'd play games and have a bonfire. There was usually a pickup game of football happening too. That year, I was a junior. Jason was a senior. Oliver and Arlan were both back from college. Portia and I were hanging out a lot by then. Like I said. I considered her my girlfriend, so, of course, I invited her to the party."

He picked up a rock and threw it out toward the lake. This next part wasn't easy to share.

"About halfway through the afternoon, I couldn't find her. Two of her cheer friends were there, so I asked if they'd seen her. They acted kind of funny and vague, and when I left the room, I heard them giggling. One of them whispered a little too loudly, 'He's such a doof. He doesn't even know the only reason she's hanging with him is so she could come to this party and get to Oliver.'"

"No way. That wasn't true, was it?" Fiona reached over and touched his arm.

He'd been wanting to touch her all day but had determined to take things slow. That gentle touch crumbled all his defenses. He covered her hand with his, locking her hand to him. He struggled to remember her question. Oh, right. Was it true?

"'Fraid so. A few minutes later, I found her and Oliver having a make-out session in the boat house. I kind of lost it. Couldn't believe either of them would do that to me. Arlan had just bought a new Indian Roadmaster. He'd driven it that day and left the keys in it. I jumped on it and started riding. Headed up the ridge into the mountains."

"Chase. Was that when . . .?"

"Yup. That was it—my big accident. I lost control on one of the curves and spun out. I don't remember anything after that for at least two weeks. A family in a minivan found me. They almost ran over the bike where it was lying on the road. They spotted me down an incline where I'd fallen, unconscious and bloody. I spent the next two weeks in a coma and the next six months in physical therapy."

"What happened with Portia and Oliver?"

He shrugged. "Oliver claimed he didn't know we'd been dating. Portia had come on to him, and back then, he wasn't one to say no if a pretty girl wanted to kiss him, whether he was interested in her or not. I never bothered to confront Portia about it. Didn't see the point. By the time I was anywhere near back to normal, she had graduated and left Wild Rose Ridge. The first time I saw her since all that went down was at the Opening Night party out at High Ridge."

"Did she mention it at all?"

"No. And I wasn't about to bring it up. It's all water under the bridge now."

They were sitting shoulder to shoulder by now. He still kept her hand clasped in his. Slowly, she turned her head and angled toward him until their lips touched.

Any final defenses crumbled immediately. He brought his hand behind her head, pulling her closer, deepening the kiss. Like their first kiss, he wasn't sure he'd could ever get enough. Kissing her was far too easy and way too addicting. Finally, he forced himself to pull away.

"Sorry. That was probably meant to be a pity kiss, and I took it way too far."

She swatted his shoulder. "That wasn't a pity kiss, Chase Coleman. That was an 'I like you' kiss." She leaned in again, her lips inches from his. "And I'd really, really like it if you'd kiss me that way again."

How was a guy to refuse an offer like that? Taking things slow was no longer even remotely on his radar.

Chapter Ten

Two days after the trip to the island, Fiona was still daydreaming about that kiss. Well, in actuality, *those* kisses. Several on the island itself. A few more on the boat. Another on the dock, and the last one out in front of the bookstore when Chase walked her home. Mmmm. She could easily spend the rest of her days kissing Chase Coleman here, there, and everywhere. She couldn't wait to see him again. Their work schedules didn't mesh at all yesterday. He'd hinted at maybe stopping by after the clinic closed later tonight. He was free this morning, but she had a podcast scheduled in an hour with Adele Langley and Ivy.

Adele and her husband were back in town. They had come to see the play on closing night and were staying to visit for a few days with old neighbors and friends. Fiona had asked Adele to be a guest on the podcast today to discuss how they'd found material for the new version of the play. Maybe if the townspeople heard about Tehya's diary and the love letters they'd found, they'd be less critical of the changes. Not that there had been much criticism. Just two separate letters to the editor. Like Chase had predicted, some people didn't like change. She knew that. She might never win those people over, but that didn't mean she wouldn't try.

The bell above the door jangled as Ivy walked in carrying her Magic Beans cup of vanilla latte. Fiona didn't begrudge her friend her daily coffee fix. Ivy was a staunch supporter of Fiona's tea shop, even though coffee was her first love.

"Have you seen the latest copy of *Remarkable News*?" Ivy asked as she threaded her way through the clusters of seating areas toward the tea bar.

"No. Is there another letter to the editor?"

"Worse. Portia wrote an op-ed piece about the play." Ivy slammed the paper onto the counter with it opened to the editorial section.

"I'm guessing she wasn't our biggest fan?"

"She isn't *your* fan, that's for sure."

Fiona glanced at the headline Ivy was pointing to. **Does Wild Rose Ridge Need to Change?** It didn't take a Rhodes Scholar to figure out whom she was referencing with that jab.

"Looks like the gloves are off on our little political battle."

"I'd say. Read it."

Fiona picked up the paper. Something told her all the memories of Chase's kisses in the world wouldn't keep this day from going south. Reluctantly, she read:

I've lived in Wild Rose Ridge my entire life. When people ask me where I'm from, I'm proud to tell them The

Ridge is my hometown. I love it here. I love the beauty of our community tucked here between the mountain ridges like a jewel in the Thorn River Valley crown. But most of all, I love the people. Personally, I can't imagine anyone wanting to live anywhere else.

That's why it puzzles me when someone says they want to change things around here. What needs to change? Our charming Main Street with its shops and eateries? The wineries, orchards, and sheer natural beauty that draw thousands of visitors to our valley each year? Maybe it's the sense of community and town pride you'll find in your neighbors and friends. Or perhaps our school system that is second to none in the state?

Frankly, I'm amazed anyone would find anything that needs changing in Wild Rose Ridge. Obviously, Fiona Jones does. Not only is she running for city council on a platform of change, but she's already changed a town institution: The Wild Rose Ridge community play. Apparently, the old version wasn't good enough for her. No matter that it has been performed the very same way for over fifty years. Sure, the plot is predictable, and the language a bit hackneyed. Yes, some of the characters might be one-dimensional, but therein lies its charm.

How many of us homegrown Wild Rose Ridgers have performed in that play? Why, I'm guessing many of us could recite whole portions of it. If you were to gather five or more of us together, we could probably act out the entire play without rehearsing. That's community. That's tradition. Shared memories and friendships. Roots that run deep and make us all strong. And that's something I'm willing to fight for.

Is it truly Time for Change *here in Wild Rose Ridge? I, for one, hope not.*

This was so unfair. Portia made it sound like Fiona didn't have all those same feelings for Wild Rose Ridge. She loved the town just as it was. She wasn't running for city council to change everything about it. She wanted to be a part of it. To help it be the best it could be. That motto had been Chase's idea. A play on words from her podcast title, *Time for Tea with Fiona. Time for Change with Fiona* only meant a change in the city council, not in what made Wild Rose Ridge so special. A time for change from the same old families and faces who always ran this city. And probably always would.

The bell on the door jangled again, bringing in both Benedict and Adele Langley this time. It was time to record the podcast. Fiona handed the paper back to Ivy and pasted on a smile for Adele. She wasn't going to let Portia's barbs unsettle her. Not today. There would be time for a rebuttal later. Maybe an answering op-ed piece. If Portia could write one, she should be able to. For now, they had a podcast to do. And, since the three of them would be talking about the play today, maybe she could use this as an opportunity to explain why they'd changed it. It could be a start, anyway.

She, Ivy, and Adele settled into the recording studio in her office and opened the podcast with the usual tea and book talk. She'd chosen Shakespeare's *As You Like It* for discussion today. She thought a play would be a fitting topic since they would talk about the festival play later. Also, Adele had been the former high school English lit teacher. Who better to discuss Shakespeare than a former

English teacher? The tea for the day was The Rosalind—a woodsy, spicy blend with a touch of sweetness.

After a lively discussion of Orlando's awful poetry and words that rhyme with Rosalind, Fiona segued into the interview portion of the podcast.

"Normally," she told the audience, "I would be the one interviewing our guest today, but since our topic is how we came about creating *Where the Wild Roses Bloom*, the play Adele and I wrote together, we thought it would be fun to let Ivy interview us. So, Ivy, why don't you take it from here?"

"Thank you, Fiona. I'd be glad to. As those of you in the audience know, the play *Where the Wild Roses Bloom* was performed five times during Wild Rose Days. Judging from the sold-out performances and the rave reviews in both *Remarkable News* and *The Wenatchee World,* I think we can safely say the play was a success. We are fortunate to have on our show today both Adele Langley and Fiona Jones, the co-writers of the play. As Fiona mentioned earlier, it's good to have Adele, or Mrs. Langley, as most of us WRRHS grads would say, back in town for a few days."

Ivy turned toward Adele. "Tell me, Mrs. Langley, what did you think of how the play turned out when you saw it for the first time Saturday night?"

"I was blown away. Honestly, when Fiona and I wrote the scenes last summer and fall, I knew it had the potential to be a great story, but to see it acted out . . . well, it all came alive for me. The actors and you, Fiona, as director, did an amazing job of telling Tehya's and Jakob's stories."

"So, walk us back," Ivy said. "When and why did you and Fiona decide to write a different version of the play? There's been some pushback from some of our Wild Rose Ridgers—not a lot, but some—about changing the former version. Could you speak to that? Why the change?"

Fiona could hug Ivy for bringing that up. And having Adele Langley, beloved town English teacher and librarian, answer that question was genius.

"I'd be happy to. As you may know, we got some negative feedback about our play after last year's festival. In fact, an article that ran in *Remarkable News* was picked up by the *Seattle Times*. Because the original play was written in the 1950s, some of the references to Native Americans that were common back then had become offensive to many, and rightly so. The Festival Committee approached me about making changes to the script, which got me thinking. Instead of simply taking out any offensive language, why not update the play altogether? Make it more appealing to a modern audience."

Adele glanced over at Fiona and smiled.

"I knew Fiona shared my love of Wild Rose Ridge history. We had been talking after one of our rehearsals last year about some primary source material we'd both recently come across. I had found Tehya's diary in a box of books sent to our library from the old Indian School library on the Yakama Reservation. And Fiona, you had found the letters, right?"

"Yes. Tehya's letters to Jakob Kohlmann. I found them in your great, great aunt Edna's attic, Ivy."

"I remember. Mom had hired you to look through her books and papers for the estate sale."

"Fiona and I knew we had a gold mine in those sources. And the story they told was as heartbreaking as the original play, maybe more so since it was the truth. We thought we could make a far more realistic and poignant play from the material we had, and I think we accomplished that, if I do say so myself. Marla Mavis at *Remarkable News* seemed to agree. Her review was far more kind this year."

Ivy laughed. "That's an understatement. 'A haunting story of weight and beauty,' I believe, is how she worded it. I love that the play is based on real history. Sure, some of it is my personal family history, so it's fascinating that way, also. But something about it being based on a true story rather than a legend made the play so much more compelling to me. And it's brought up a few things that I didn't know happened like our family sharing our grape vines with the Bouchard family. My Grandpa Ben always said those Lemberger vines were never theirs, but Tehya's version was confirmed for me by something else you found recently. Right, Fiona?"

"You're talking about Wilhelm Kohlmann's journal? Yes. It does confirm the sharing of the grape vines. It also confirms the fight between the two families and the building of the wall, just like in the play."

"You found Wilhelm Kohlmann's journal?" Adele had always loved to hear about Fiona's historical finds. "You didn't tell me that."

"That and several other documents the Coleman family has wanted to locate. One of them happened to be the final letter from Tehya to Jakob. We used it at the end of the play."

"That explains so much," Adele said. "I loved how you added that narration to the last scene, but I had no idea it was authentic. We always wondered how it ended, didn't we? And now we know. In actuality, we weren't too far from the truth. But where did you find that letter?"

"In Rob and Darlene Coleman's attic, hidden way in the back behind a knee wall. The letter itself was stuck down in the spine of a first edition *Ben Hur* we'd found in Jakob Kohlmann's old trunk."

"A first edition *Ben Hur*? Oh, I'm going to have to see that." Adele's enthusiasm for all things literary was what Fiona missed most about her friend.

"You'll love it," she responded. "It's in prime condition and has Jakob's name written on the flyleaf. You'll want to see the hand-drawn map we found too. Oh, and Ivy, did I tell you? We found enough evidence to prove your Grandpa Ben was not totally wrong. Those Lemberger vines never did belong to the Morales family. At least not the ones they claim to be theirs now."

Ivy gasped. "You found the deed?"

Fiona found herself getting caught up in her friend's excitement. "Yes. And even more than that. Physical proof that the boundary to your uncle's property is not anywhere near where the Morales family claims it is. Those Lemberger vines they are so proud of aren't on their property and never were."

"This is huge." Ivy started out of her chair, then stopped midway, eyes growing big, face turning white. Fiona realized their blunder at the exact same moment. They were still on the air. They weren't sitting at her kitchen table talking about the attic exploration as they'd done so many times before. This time, everything they'd said had been broadcast to anyone in Wild Rose Ridge who had tuned in this morning. This was more than huge. It was disastrous.

Ivy recovered far more quickly than Fiona did. She cued the show's theme music.

"And that's all the time we have for today, everyone," she said. "I'd like to thank Mrs. Langley . . . Adele, for joining us here today. It's been such a delight. Now, remember everyone, the secret to a well-balanced life is a cup of tea in one hand and a good book in the other. See you next week on *Time for Tea with Fiona*."

Ivy switched off the microphone and slumped back in her chair. Fiona covered her face with her hands and groaned.

"What did we just do?"

"Opened a huge can of worms would be my bet." There was a hint of laughter in Adele Langley's voice. But then, she wasn't the one who had to deal with the repercussions of this. What would Chase say?

"Can we edit it?" Ivy asked. "Take that last bit out before we upload it?"

"I have it set to upload automatically, but we can edit it. I think. I've never done it before." She had never let her big mouth get away with itself on air until now. Why, why, why couldn't she have kept her mouth shut about the boundary dispute?

"We could take it down." Ivy started frantically typing something into the computer. "What's the administrative password again?"

"It's already been broadcast live, am I correct? Taking

it down might cause more talk than leaving it." Adele spoke with a voice of reason. "I'm guessing you have a pretty faithful audience who tunes in live? I know I always tried to listen on Tuesday mornings when I lived here. I've fallen a little off schedule since moving to San Diego, but knowing this town, I'd say the damage is probably already done."

Fiona's phone buzzed. She glanced at the screen and groaned again. "I'd say you're right."

She showed Ivy and Adele the name on the screen. Marla Mavis from *Remarkable News*. No way she was calling simply to chat. Fiona ignored the call and put her phone on silent. A few seconds later, Ivy's phone buzzed. She grimaced when she looked at the screen.

"Marla?" Fiona asked.

"Worse. My mom. I better take this." As Ivy stepped out of the room, Fiona could hear her saying, "Yes. I know, Mom. It's huge."

Fiona leaned back in her chair. "What are we going to do?"

"I'm not sure there is anything you can do. Is anything you said untrue?" Adele's reasonable tone was calming.

"No."

"Then let it run its course. With half the town being related to either a Morales or a Coleman, this would get out in a few days anyway. If it's anything like their last boundary dispute from the 90s, the minute Rob Coleman brings up the matter with the county auditor, things will go pear-shaped super fast. Trust me. Whether this news hits today or a few days down the road, the result will be the same. Everyone will be in an uproar for a while, and then it will all die down when the next bit of town drama comes along."

Easy for Adele to say. She wasn't the one who blabbed her boyfriend's family secret to the entire town. If he even *was* her boyfriend. They'd never officially called themselves boyfriend and girlfriend. After this, that might never happen. Those kisses, wonderful as they were, might be the last ones they shared.

Fiona glanced at her phone. Seven o'clock. The clinic closed an hour and a half ago. Even if Chase had a pile of paperwork or an appointment that ran late, he should have been free by now to at least text her, especially since she had sent no less than fourteen texts to him over the course of the day.

They'd started simple with an I'm sorry and gradually become more frantic and incoherent the longer he was silent. She was totally blowing this, and she knew it. But somehow, she couldn't stop. What also wouldn't stop were all the texts and phone messages coming in from townspeople who had heard her podcast. Or heard about it from someone who had heard it.

The chat room on BuzzSprout had blown up the minute they went off the air. Normally, she and Ivy would stick around and answer questions and feedback after a broadcast. Today, she shut it all down. She didn't trust herself not to say more than she should say on the topic. Until she talked to Chase, she was lying low. She hadn't even taken her turn at the tea counter today, bribing Katie Rose to cover her afternoon and evening shift. Sometimes, paying your employees double was worth it.

Although she hadn't responded to any comments in the chat room or any texts, she had read them. They ranged anywhere from OMG. ARE YOU SERIOUS? I KNEW THE MORALES FAMILY WERE CHEATS to WHAT A TERRIBLE WAY TO TRY TO WIN VOTES! HOW CAN YOU POSSIBLY THINK SPREADING LIES ABOUT ONE OF WILD ROSE RIDGE'S MOST LOVED FAMILIES IS GOING TO HELP YOUR CAMPAIGN IN ANY WAY?

At least Marla Mavis had stopped calling. She must have found another source for the news article that was sure to appear in tomorrow's issue of *Remarkable News*. Ivy and Adele left shortly after the broadcast. Fiona had shut herself in her office and done her best to lose herself in spreadsheets and balances. Not that she was at all successful. The numbers part of the business was her least favorite part. It certainly wasn't going to keep her mind off Chase and how he was going to react to her spreading the news about the deed to the entire community. As far as she knew, he hadn't even told his parents about the deed yet.

Fiona shut down her computer. Maybe going through that box of old books Benedict had left on her desk this morning would take her mind off things. At least until closing time. She picked up the first volume, a 1914 edition of *The Flaming Sword*. She didn't recognize the title but scanning the first few pages, she identified it as a typical adventure novel popular in the early 20th

century. They were a little sensational but sometimes fun to read.

She was scanning through the first chapter when Katie Rose flung open the door to her office. "Jeremy just texted me. He says Franco Morales and Rob Coleman got into a big fight, and Mr. Coleman dropped down dead."

All the air fled the room. Fiona struggled to breathe, to think, to move. Dead! No. No, no. Please, God. No. Let this be a dream.

Her phone started vibrating on her desk, and Fiona glanced at the screen. Ivy.

She fumbled to pick it up and answer the call. "Please tell me it isn't true."

Ivy's tear-filled voice came back. "It is. They've life-flighted him to Harborview in Seattle. Mom's on her way there now."

"Then he's not dead?"

"Dead? Oh God, no. I don't think so. He had a heart attack but was alive when they put him on the helicopter. Chase is with him. Why? What did you hear?"

"Nothing. I'm sure whatever I heard was all blown out of proportion. What can I do?"

"Pray. Please, just pray."

"I will. You know I will. And Ivy? Let me know as soon as you hear anything."

Fiona turned to Katie, who still stood in the doorway. "He's not dead. He's had a heart attack. He's on his way to Harborview. Tell the others that and pray."

As Katie left, Fiona dropped her head onto the desk and let the tears flow. *Please, God. Please. Don't let him die.*

Chapter Eleven

In the four years he'd been practicing medicine, the last twenty hours had to have been the most brutal. Then again, Chase had never had to be both doctor and son to a patient before. Especially not in a life-and-death situation. Fighting for a man's life was one thing. Fighting for his father's life was another level entirely.

That wasn't the worst part. The very worst part of this whole ordeal had to be the four hours Dad was in emergency surgery, and he had no idea how things were going or any input into his care. He'd spent those hours searching scripture for some comfort and praying. Or at least trying to. To be perfectly honest, his prayers often turned into worry about how things were going in the operating room. Guess he had a little of Oliver's need to control things, after all. Maybe he was more like his big brother than he thought.

It wasn't that Chase hadn't trusted Dr. Stevens. According to his partner, Stan Johnson, Dr. Richard

Stevens was one of the best cardiologists in the state. Chase was neither a cardiologist nor a surgeon. He knew he had needed to hand that part off. With any other patient, it would have been easy. Nothing was easy when the patient was your father.

Thank goodness for his training as an emergency room physician, though. It must have been a God thing that he'd even been there when Dad needed him last evening. He was planning to spend all his time after work with Fiona but decided to swing by Rose Cove at the last minute before heading to the tea shop. He wanted to tell his parents about the deed. Bring them up to speed on what George Hardin had told him. He'd arrived at the barn the moment Dad collapsed. Thankfully, he'd been able to keep him stable until the EMTs showed up.

Now, almost twenty hours later, Dad was finally out of the woods. After a triple bypass, he'd have a long road to recovery, but his life was no longer in danger. Chase had left Mom by Dad's bedside and headed down to the lobby for some much-needed coffee.

He'd just turned away from the coffee kiosk with a plain Americano in hand when he heard a familiar voice.

"Dad must be doing well if the doctor's taking a coffee break."

"Oliver." Chase gave his big brother a hug and a slap on the back. "Glad you could make it. When did you get in?"

"About an hour ago. I rented a car and came straight over. I saw Aunt Violet and Uncle Steve in the parking lot just now, so I got the update. The surgery went well?"

"Yes. Dad's still sedated, but he should become more

alert within an hour or two. Mom's with him now. Come on. I'll show you to the family waiting room."

Chase took Oliver to the small sitting room outside Dad's ICU room. The room had been full of family most of the night but had cleared out now that Dad was out of surgery and resting.

"Mom will probably want to know you're here," he said.

"Leave her for now. Take me through what happened last night."

"What did Aunt Violet tell you?"

"Pretty much what Mom had texted throughout the night. Dad had an emergency triple bypass early this morning and is now stable. I wanted to know more about the heart attack itself. How did it happen?"

"I'm not sure of the details. I drove to Rose Cove yesterday after work to visit with Mom and Dad. I saw a lot of commotion over by the barn, so I headed there first. Found Dad down on the ground with no heartbeat. I was able to get his heart started before the EMTs got there. Then, with Stan Johnson's advice, we were able to life-flight him here to be under the care of Dr. Stevens and his team. Stan tells me he's the best cardiologist in central Washington. Ranked among the best in the state. I'm convinced he saved Dad's life last night."

Oliver raked a hand through his hair. "Wow. I hadn't expected this. Dad's only in his late fifties. Too young to be almost dying of a heart attack. It's that stupid vineyard. The stress is going to kill him if he doesn't get out from under it. We're going to have to convince him to sell."

"I disagree. The vineyard is his home. Selling it will

cause a lot more stress than keeping it will. He'll need to find more help in the vines, especially this summer and fall, but his vintner work in the winery could be very therapeutic. He loves doing that. And after he recovers from his surgery, which should take about twelve weeks, he'll be able to return to the vineyard work too. As long as he gets on a good diet and exercise regimen."

Oliver shook his head. "Listen to you sounding all doctor-y and everything. Too bad you couldn't have seen this coming and headed it off before it happened." That comment hit a little too close to the recriminations Chase had been sending himself all night. He should have pushed Dad harder about getting that checkup. But Oliver never seemed to notice when his jabs drew blood. He simply continued talking. "Face it, Chase. There have never been enough workers to help Dad run Rose Cove. Besides, none of us kids are ever going to take it over. He might as well be rid of it now."

Typical Oliver. Coming into a middle of a situation and thinking he alone knew how to solve it.

"I think it's way too premature to talk about selling Mom and Dad's home and livelihood. Dad does have the final say in that, you know. He's had a heart attack, but he's not incapacitated. Let him heal, and then you can talk options with him." Like Dad would ever willingly sell Rose Cove.

"You honestly think he's going to be fine running the vineyard and dealing with a lengthy property line battle on top of all that? Do you even know how much debt he accumulated investing in all his winery equipment? If he doesn't have a good harvest this year, he's done. He certainly doesn't have the money it will take to fight the Morales family again in court."

"Who said anything about a court battle? Where are you getting your information?"

"Jason. Arlan. Just about everyone in Wild Rose Ridge. It's all the town can talk about. How some girl named Fiona called the Morales family a bunch of thieves to win votes for her city council run. She said they'd stolen the Lemberger vines. Then, when Franco confronted Dad about it, Dad keeled over in a heart attack."

Chase stared at Oliver. Had he gone mad? What in the world was he talking about? And how did he know about Fiona? Or the property line battle?

"That doesn't sound at all like something Fiona would do."

"Oh, great. Don't tell me. You're involved with this Fiona girl somehow. Why does that not surprise me? You in a relationship with a girl who only wants to use you. When will you learn to stop picking girls who cause our family to implode?"

Now Oliver had gone way too far. Chase grabbed his brother's shirt collar with both his fists, lifted him up, and shoved him against the wall.

"Don't. Don't you ever go there again. Fiona is nothing like Portia. And if anything caused our family to implode back then, it was as much your fault as mine. So don't come waltzing in here with all your crazy solutions, playing some sort of blame game." He gave Oliver one more shove, then raised his hands and backed off. "I don't have time for this. I have a consultation meeting to get to, and then I'm going home to sleep. In case you didn't know, instead of trying to find all sorts of people and things to blame for this, I've spent the past twenty hours trying to save Dad's life. You're welcome."

He stormed from the room, nearly bowling over Ivy, who stood in the hallway clutching a drink in both hands while balancing a potted plant on her hip.

"What just ha—"

"Sorry, Ivy," he cut her off as he reached out to steady her. "I'd stay to talk, but I'm late for my meeting with Dad's team of surgeons. Feel free to reconnect with Oliver, though. He's a bundle of fun."

Chase strode down the hall, letting his anger build and fuel him. Oliver hadn't changed a bit. Always thinking he knew best. Well, when it came to Dad's care, Chase knew better this time. And if Oliver thought he was going to convince Dad to sell the property that had been in their family for five generations, then Chase would be there to fight him all the way.

This was a really bad idea. Fiona didn't know why she'd allowed Ivy to talk her into it. Yet, here she was, walking down the hallway of the ICU unit carrying a small, potted philodendron. Ivy had stopped to get them both drinks at the coffee kiosk downstairs, but Fiona knew that if she waited, she might never have the courage to continue. They'd seen Chase and his brother Oliver disappear into the elevators just as they entered the lobby.

Ivy had told her they were probably headed for the family waiting room next to Rob Coleman's hospital room. Fiona wasn't family, but she was with Ivy, who was, so that counted, right?

"I'm going to try to catch up with Chase," she'd told Ivy. "See you up there?"

"I'll be right behind you."

She'd told the nurse on duty at the nurse's station that she was with Chase and Oliver Coleman and had been waved toward an open doorway halfway down the hall. As she drew closer to the room, her steps grew slower. Maybe she should have waited for Ivy after all. What if Chase was angry with her? Ivy had told her he wasn't, but what did she know? This was Ivy's first visit as well.

"We'll go together," she had told Fiona that morning. "We both were a part of that podcast and equally responsible for talking about the deed on air. We'll both go. Let them know how sorry we are. It'll be fine. You'll see."

But what if it wasn't? What if the entire Coleman family treated her the way all the others in Wild Rose Ridge had today? With side-eyed glances, whispers, and outright avoidance? She didn't think her heart could take it if Chase rejected her.

She came to the waiting room and heard Chase's voice inside the room. He sounded angry. She paused a minute to gather her courage. She could do this. This was Chase. The one who kissed her senseless three days ago. She could trust him.

She started forward in time to hear Oliver say, "Don't

tell me. You're involved with this Fiona girl somehow. Right? Why does that not surprise me? You, in a relationship with a girl who only wants to use you. When will you learn to stop picking girls who cause our family to implode?"

Oh, God. It was exactly what she feared. Chase's family hated her. She turned to find Ivy right behind her. Shoving the plant into Ivy's already full arms, she turned and fled. She wasn't brave enough to face them today. Maybe she never would be.

Ten minutes later, she was in her car speeding up I-90 toward Wild Rose Ridge. For the first time ever, she dreaded going home. Home. Would she ever find a place that was truly home? She thought she had found it, but once again, she was on the outside looking in on a community that had turned its back on her.

She let the tears flow.

God, why? Why has there never been a place for me? Why can't I ever fit in?

Her phone rang through the speaker on her dashboard. She reached over to hang up the call until she saw the name on the screen.

"Dad?"

"Hi, honey."

"What is it? Is something wrong? Why are you calling so late? It is late there, right?" Her brain struggled to do the math.

Dad chuckled. "Yeah. Not as late as Kenya time. Your mom and I are in Brussels for a conference this week. But, yeah. It's about 1 a.m. here. Don't worry. I'm fine. Your mom's fine. It's just . . ." He paused for a minute.

When he continued, his voice sounded a little tentative. "It's just that I had this sense that you are not fine. I've been up praying. Couldn't sleep. And you came to mind. So I thought I'd call. Is this a bad time?"

"No." The word came out as a squeak as the tears flowed even harder.

"I hear tears, Redbud. What's wrong?"

"Everything." Between hiccups and sobs, she managed to parcel out the events of the last day and a half, from blurting the Coleman's secret on air to how the town reacted to her after Rob Coleman's heart attack. "They hate me. And I don't blame them. I almost killed him. And Chase . . . Chase will never forgive me."

"Hold on there. Something tells me you're taking on a lot more guilt for all this than is warranted. Sure, you let your mouth run a bit when you shouldn't have, but your actions aren't to blame for Rob Coleman's heart attack. If the man had to have emergency bypass surgery, that heart attack would have happened sooner or later."

"But the town hates me. There's no way any of them will vote for me as city councilwoman now. Everywhere I go, it's the same. I can't seem to find a place I belong."

Dad was silent for a long time. Had they lost their connection? But then, his voice came over the car speaker again.

"Redbud, I think you're looking for home in all the wrong places. Home is not a specific place or an entire community. If you're looking for home in the acceptance and favor of all the people around you, you'll be disappointed every time. Even Jesus, perfect man, didn't achieve that. He never meant to.

"But that's not what it means to belong. Belonging is finding those people whose life you impact while they impact yours. You do belong. You've belonged in my heart and your mother's since the day you were conceived. Since then, you've impacted lives wherever we lived. Remember Kali?"

"I was three, Dad."

"Yes. And even then, you made an impact. That day you got lost in the jungle, the entire village showed up to search for you. They loved the little girl with the big smile and hair of fire. That's exactly how their village chief, Mugisa, put it.

"And then there's, Dembe, Asamo, and Masiko. Every time I see them, they ask about you. Mimi and PopPop. You don't think you made an impact there? You're a lucky girl to have pockets of community all over the world."

She'd never felt lucky. She'd felt lonely. The odd man out who didn't quite fit into any culture or community. But Dad had a point. There were individuals all over the world she loved. And they loved her.

"Even more important than that," Dad continued. " You've belonged in the family of God since the moment you believed in God's grace. That's where you find your acceptance. That's where you find your worth. Would you do me a favor, Redbud?"

"What?"

"When you get a chance, look up John 15 and read it in the Message. That's the passage where Jesus talks about being the vine. He tells us to make our home in Him. That's a home and belonging that never disappoints

Chapter Twelve

Chase walked back into Dad's hospital room early the next morning to find him in a Facetime conversation with a teary-eyed Tori.

"Chase is here," Dad said. He turned his phone in Chase's direction. "Tell her I'm fine. Tell her she doesn't need to schedule a flight home."

"Dad's fine, Tori. He'll need to take it easy for a while, but he should be back to his old self in twelve weeks. Save your travel money for Christmas."

"But what about the vineyard? Won't he need help with the harvest?"

"Oliver's home now," Dad said. "He and I will work with Pete to get all that figured out. Don't you worry. It's time Oliver started taking a bigger interest in the family business anyway."

Yeah. Good luck with that.

Chase hadn't slept much, a couple of hours at the most. The rest of the night, he'd tossed and turned, still burning at some of the things Oliver had said. What gave him the right to waltz in here and decide Dad needed to sell Rose Cove? What worried Chase most was that Dad had always deferred to Oliver. Oliver was his golden boy. What if Oliver convinced Dad to sell?

No way. Chase would fight tooth and nail before he let that happen. Oliver wasn't the only voice in what happened to the family legacy.

"I better go now, sweetheart," Dad said to Tori. "The doctor's here to check me over." He sent Chase a wink. Chase could already tell his father was feeling much better. He'd still need his rest, but recovery was well underway.

"All right, Daddy. I love you. And Chase? Thank you. Mom says Dad wouldn't be here if it weren't for you." The last was said on the edge of a sob.

Chase gave a nod, not knowing how to respond to that. "Take care, Tori," he said. "We'll talk soon."

Dad shut down the call and turned to Chase. "She's right, you know. I owe you my life, son."

Chase's throat tightened as he struggled to control his emotions. Dad didn't need another of his children crying all over him this morning.

"We both know I'm not the one to thank," he finally said. "I didn't just happen to be in the right place at the right time Tuesday night. That was totally a God thing."

"And I've been praising Him for it. But it was your actions that saved me. You have a gift, son. Don't downplay it. Mom tells me she found great comfort in the calm, cool way you handled everything."

"It *is* my job, Dad."

"But I'm your father. I'm sure that made everything

harder. I should have listened to you. You told me several times that I needed a check-up, but I was stubborn and pushed ahead anyway. I'm sorry I put you through that."

"And I should have insisted. I got so caught up with the play, and Fiona, and finding the deed—"

"The deed? That's right! I remember now. Franco was yelling something about a deed when I came into the barn last night. What was that all about?"

"You don't know? I thought you were arguing with him."

"Not that I recall. I had been feeling off all afternoon. Lightheaded and dizzy. Even a little nauseous. I thought I might be dehydrated. I'd had spells like that before, but usually, rest and a water bottle or two would be all I needed. Anyway, I walked into the barn and suddenly had the most severe pain in my chest I'd ever experienced. I don't remember anything after that until I came to on the way to the hospital. So what did Franco want? Did you find our old deed?"

"I did. Up in the attic. It was in the last section I looked through in an old trunk. I was coming to tell you and Mom all about it last evening."

"I'm guessing, from all of Franco's bluster, it proved our side of the story?" Dad suddenly looked very tired. "I suppose that means another court battle."

"Not necessarily. George Hardin at the county auditor's office spotted some discrepancies in the deed the Morales family produced for the first court case. Comparing it to ours, which he said was the real deal, makes theirs looks pretty fishy. He thinks that if we had our lawyer show their lawyer the evidence we've found, they would realize they don't have a case and be willing to settle. But we can talk about that after you are better. Right now, you need your rest. Did Mom and Oliver leave?"

Dad shook his head. "I sent them out for breakfast. I wanted to send your mom home, but she'll have none of it. I know she didn't sleep well on that couch over there last night, but she's a stubborn one."

Chase smiled. "I'll talk to them when they get back. Make sure they know we need to limit visitors for a while. How's your pain level? Do I need to ask for more meds?"

"I'm fine. They put something in my I.V. right before Tori called."

Chase could tell by the way Dad was beginning to slur his words that the drugs were starting to take effect.

"Good. I'll leave you to sleep, then. I'll check back again in a few hours."

"Chase?" Dad grabbed his hand as he turned to go. "I could not be prouder of you than I am right now. I'm blessed to call you son."

Wow. Dad had never said anything like that to him before. Mom, yes, but never Dad. Anytime he'd ever said he was proud of someone, it had always been Oliver. Of course, Chase had always been the screwup when they were kids. Right up until the motorcycle accident. But since the accident, all those years of schooling, working toward his goals. It was as if Dad hadn't noticed. Chase hadn't realized how much he'd longed to hear those words from his father until now. He couldn't respond without bursting into tears, so he squeezed Dad's hand and nodded.

Dad's eyes drifted closed as Chase made his way out of the room. The anger and guilt he'd felt coming into the hospital this morning dissipated. The truth was he was not to blame for his father's heart attack. The truth was his father *did* see and value him. The truth was he'd been granted more time on this earth with his father around.

Life was good. *God* was good.

He pulled his phone from his pocket and sent a text to Fiona.

Fiona sat on the end of the dock, letting her feet dangle above the crystal-clear water of Wild Rose Lake. Any other time, she would be soothed by the quiet beauty of this place. The sapphire blue water. The golden glow of the late afternoon sun. How often had she sat in this very spot to think, pray, and dream? But today, her thoughts were in such a snarl that no beauty could calm them.

Meet me at the dock—6 p.m.

That was the one and only text she'd received from Chase since early Tuesday morning. Granted, forty-eight hours ago, his father had suffered a major heart attack. On top of that was the fact that other than those kisses on Sunday, they were not officially anything more than good friends. It wasn't like he owed her a phone call or a text. Ivy had told her that he wasn't mad at her, but why hadn't he called if that was the case? You would think the fifteen texts she'd sent him, each more frantic than the one before it, would have elicited some sort of response. But, nothing. Until this morning when he'd sent those cryptic words.

Meet me at the dock—6 p.m.

She supposed he meant today. She also supposed he meant this dock. The one where he'd asked her to sail with him all those years ago. The one where they shared their first kiss. But what if he didn't? Was she at the wrong place? On the wrong day?

And then she saw him. Time slowed to a complete stop until he caught sight of her and grinned. With that grin, her whole world righted. Suddenly, the lake had never looked bluer. The air had never felt clearer. The birdsong had never sounded so sweet. That grin turned her way, meant only for her, had the power to unsnarl any knot her errant thoughts had tangled.

He walked down the dock toward her carrying a box of Crusty's Pizza. Truly. Had any man ever looked so good? He was dressed casually—sandals, board shorts, and a t-shirt that molded to his chest and shoulders. His hair was damp as if he'd just come from the shower. He smelled good, too, like cedar and citrus. She drew in a deep whiff of him as he sat down beside her.

"Hey," he said, his voice low and warm.

"Hey."

She stared at him a moment, then plunged in. "Chase, I'm so sorry about your father. I don't know if you got all my texts, but I never meant to talk about the deed on air. Ivy and I got so caught up in our conversation that we totally forgot we were on the podcast. I swear I never—"

Chase placed a finger on her lips, sending tingles through her. His half grin was almost as potent as his full one. "Shhh," he said. "I know. It's fine. I did get your texts. All of them."

She felt her face burn at the laughter in his eyes. Okay. Fine. Some of those last few texts had gotten pretty crazy. She'd read them back after he'd sent her the text about meeting him here. She'd been embarrassed by how psychotic she had sounded. Honestly, it's a wonder he'd shown up here at all. And that he didn't look at all mad. He even looked like he was happy to see her.

"You didn't respond." Like that didn't sound like a sulky child. Come on, Fiona. Get a grip.

He had the decency to look a little guilty. "I know. I'm sorry. I meant to call you earlier today, but I crashed when I got home from seeing Dad this morning. To be honest, I hadn't had much sleep until then. I just woke up half an hour ago. So, I figured it would be easier to say everything face to face than to try to put it all in a text. First off, what's this all about?" He picked up a folded newspaper he had sat on top of the pizza box.

Oh. Marla's latest article had appeared in this afternoon's copy of *Remarkable News*.

Fiona shrugged. "I withdrew from the council race."

"But why? I hope it's not because of Dad and those silly rumors about you trying to bring down the Morales family because of Portia."

"No. Actually, it's all because of me. I realized something yesterday. I never really wanted to be a city councilwoman. Don't get me wrong. I still love Wild Rose Ridge and will do anything to support the people here. But I don't want to be the one deciding how to spend their taxes and telling them what to do. I'm not sure why I ever thought I did."

"This isn't about Portia, then?"

"No. I'd take Portia on in a heartbeat if I truly wanted the job. The fact is, I'm glad Portia joined the race for city council. It showed me something I didn't realize before. I'm not a politician, and I don't want to be. I thought being a councilwoman was my path to truly belonging here in Wild Rose Ridge, but you know what? I think I already do belong."

"I'm glad to hear that because I totally agree."

"But, Chase. Tell me about your father. I know he's doing better, but you can't imagine how sorry I am that something I said led to his heart attack."

"That's just it. It didn't. In typical small-town fashion, Wild Rose Ridge blew that one way out of proportion. Dad didn't even know about the deed until I told him about it after his surgery. He saw Franco at the barn that night but barely remembers what he said. His mind was focused on his pain and what was happening to his body. He would have had the heart attack even if Franco hadn't been there."

"Really?"

"Really."

All that guilt. All the angst. All those tears. Turns out, it was nothing but an overblown piece of Wild Rose Ridge gossip. Another example of how the townspeople could make mountains out of molehills.

She laughed and shook her head.

"I know," Chase said. "I felt all sorts of guilty for not telling him about finding the deed sooner. The fact is it wasn't anyone's fault. He had a heart attack because he had a diseased heart. Plain and simple."

"But he's doing okay?"

"He's doing great."

"And your family doesn't hate me?"

"My family? Oh, you mean Oliver. Ivy told me you overheard our argument. I'm sorry you had to hear that. Sibling relations can get ugly sometimes. Believe me, what happened that day was more about Oliver and me than it was about you. He and I still have some things to work out, but trust me, my family doesn't hate you." He reached out and caught a strand of her hair that was blowing across her face and tucked it behind her ear. "Enough about that. Let's talk about something far more important. You have the most beautiful hair I've ever seen. Have I told you that?"

She shook her head, finding it hard to break the hold of his gaze.

"I've missed you." His hand lingered on her neck, softly stroking the skin behind her ear. A shiver ran down her at his touch.

"I've missed you too."

"The last time we were on this dock, I said I hoped we could be more than friends. Remember?"

"I remember."

"And then I kissed you, and you ran away."

"I didn't run away."

"You most certainly did. Which led me to believe you didn't want to be more than friends."

"I didn't run away on Sunday. You kissed me then too."

"You're right. You didn't. Which gives me hope." Chase leaned in closer until his lips were almost touching hers. She could feel the heat from his breath as he talked. "If I were to kiss you now, would you agree to be more than friends? Like my girlfriend?"

"Maybe you should kiss me and find out."

He closed the distance then, capturing her lips and drawing her in once again. When he finally pulled away, she was glad to see him looking as dazed as she felt.

"Is that a yes, then?"

"It most definitely is a yes. And just so you know, it was a yes the first time too."

THE END

About the Author

A south-Texas transplant to the good life of Nebraska, Kathy Geary Anderson has a passion for story and all things historical. Over the years, she has been an English teacher, a newsletter and ad writer, and a stay-at-home mom. When she's not reading or writing novels, she can be found cheering (far too loudly) for her favorite football team, traveling the country with her husband, or spending time with her adult children. For more information on upcoming releases, visit www.kathygearyanderson.com

Other Books by Kathy Geary Anderson

The Trouble with Jenny

Songs in the Storm

A Refuge of Convieniance

Ready for more Wild Rose Ridge?

Check out this excerpt from Fashioned for Love, the next book in the Wild Rose Ridge Series!

Fasthioned for Love

Nina Taylor was going to win the Pacific Northwest Fashion Blogger of the Year award if it killed her. What else did she have?

Mom set her fingernail file down on the glass coffee table and examined a long, red tip. "You work hard. Too hard in my opinion." Mom *would* say. She preferred luxury over effort. Their living room was case in point.

"If I win this award, I'll get a two-page spread in Seattle Chic. It's the most popular women's magazine in the Pacific Northwest. The magazine would drive traffic to my social media accounts, especially my YouTube channel." Nina fingered the simple silver chain at her neck. "This is the break I need. I won't have to hustle waiting tables at a restaurant I can't even afford to eat at. Besides, I'm tired of working twelve-hour days."

And tired of living with Mom. But renting even a small place in Seattle was an impossible proposition. Even if Nina found a place she could afford, which she wouldn't, she'd have to have a couple of roommates to share expenses.

"I'm glad you can finally admit that you're tired. Maybe now you'll appreciate that working at Zingers is your best chance at catching the eye of a wealthy man, so you don't have to work at all." Mom pulled the gold velvet curtain back from the floor-to-ceiling windows in their twenty-seventh-floor condo overlooking Elliot Bay and Pike Place Market.

Nina stood and crossed the room to stand next to Mom at the window. "Not tired enough to quit on my dreams." Nina placed her palms on the cold glass and shivered. The gray sky reflected her mood this morning. She dropped her gaze to the bay below. It was nothing like the deep blue lake she'd spent so many happy summers on.

On a sunny day the view from the condo was gorgeous. But there weren't enough sunny days to make it worth living here. The filth and crime made Seattle a dangerous place lately. Many business owners had packed up and moved to greener pastures.

Mom was stubborn though. Living at the Emerald meant Mom had the use of the Tesla they provided. The more tedious tasks in her life were managed by their concierge, and they had a yoga studio, fitness center, and pet spa. Not that Mom would ever have a pet. The perks of ownership at the prestigious Emerald were numerous. Living in this building was not unlike living in a bubble.

They had Mom's fifth husband to thank for their swanky address, or rather the divorce settlement from him. Edward hadn't been such a bad guy. In fact, Nina almost missed him.

But she'd learned early in life not to get too attached.

A nostalgic sigh for summers spent with Aunt Shirley and Uncle Sherman in Wild Rose Ridge escaped her. She hadn't been back since Sherm's funeral. She'd gotten too busy for lakeside summers. A smile lifted Nina's mouth as memories of flirting with the local boys and working at Aunt Shirley's boutique chased away the dull grime of the city below.

Those summers were the reason she loved fashion and she was finally going back. The small town had a big spring festival to kick-off the tourist season. Aunt Shirley put on a fashion show every year. This year she'd asked Nina to manage the whole thing. The local news would make a big deal out of the festival and who knew what might come of this opportunity.

Nina sniffed on her way to the kitchen. "Is the coffee ready?"

"Just heard it beep." Mom was strapping on silver heels.

"Where are you going this early?" Nina took in Mom's figure-hugging slacks. She wore a new blouse in a blush pink shade.

"Hair appointment." Mom said in a clipped tone. Her heels clacked on the Italian marble floor as she walked to the kitchen cupboard and set two matching mugs on the gleaming marble counter. She poured two mugs of dark brew coffee. "Then a lunch date."

"Lunch date?" Nina forced herself not to cringe. Mom was notorious for turning lunch dates into quickie wedding ceremonies.

Nina folded herself into one corner of the sofa and gnawed her fingernails.

"Don't be so nosy." Mom carried the mugs into the living room and set one down on the glass topped coffee table. "Are you all packed and ready to go?"

"Leaving a week early will give me time to pick up anything I've forgotten." Nina leaned forward to take a coffee. The white leather sofa had swallowed her phone and iPad. She fished between the cushions with one hand, careful not to spill.

"Maybe you should use those few days to take a cruise or go on a wine tasting with Karoline. She'd probably appreciate experiencing Wild Rose with someone familiar with it."

"Karoline is there to work. She's going as my assistant, not my friend." Nina snagged her phone and thumbed the screen to scroll her social media.

Mom shrugged. "I just think you should schedule in a little fun." Mom checked her eye make-up in a pocket mirror.

Of course, Mom would focus on having a good time. Nina sipped her hot, bitter coffee. Oh, to have cream again. But no, she was going to stick to her diet. It was true that the camera added ten pounds and several newspaper and local camera crews would be in Wild Rose all week.

"I wish you'd come. The spring festival is kind of a big deal. You grew up there. Don't you miss it?" Nina set her mug on the coffee table and fished for her iPad.

"Small-town life was never my style. I felt trapped there." Mom's mouth pulled down in an unbecoming frown.

"Kind of how I feel here," Nina muttered.

Mom glanced at her watch, which she wore so the face was on her wrist. A very expensive gift from her third husband. Or was that the fourth?

"You'll watch my Instagram and Youtube?" Nina tried not to let that pathetic tone seep in, but there it was again.

"Of course. I said I would, didn't I?"

"You did." Nina nodded. "But sometimes you forget."

"I'm a busy woman, Nina." Mom wandered down the hallway toward her bedroom.

She'd let that one slide. Mom was busy when she was in between husbands. Busy looking for the next one.

Nina checked her "likes" and replied to comments on Instagram then moved on to YouTube. Her usual morning routine. It used to be exciting but lately it had become rote. Her phone pinged next to her on the sofa, and she glanced down to see a text from Karoline.

Can I call?

She thumbed back,

Sure

The ringtone on her phone sounded. "Hey. What's up?"

"Our Beast is in jail."

"What?"

"For real. The model we hired to be the Beast in the fashion show got into some kind of trouble. The agency won't say what kind exactly. They hinted at drugs." The note of panic in Karoline's voice leaked through the phone.

"Great." A dull throb beat behind Nina's right eye. Everything needed to be perfect. "Now we have to choose someone else. Finding a man with the exact look we want took forever."

"It's not that easy."

"Why not?" Nina demanded.

"The agency announced bankruptcy early this morning."

There was a long pause in which Nina imagined herself as a middle-aged woman still waiting tables. "How do you know?"

"I tried calling to figure out a replacement, but no one would answer so I went to their office. The receptionist for the denture clinic next door gave me the dirt on the agency."

"They were next door to a denture clinic? No wonder they went bankrupt." Nina clenched her eyes shut. Coffee burned an acid trail back up her throat.

"Nina, what are we going to do? Even if we could find another man that perfect, we couldn't afford him. We paid a deposit to the modeling agency that we'll never get back."

A great big honking deposit.

"I knew we shouldn't have paid so much." Karoline tended to panic. Not an ideal trait in an assistant.

"I didn't want to skimp." Nina defended her decision.

"The theme is beauty and the beast. We needed the best-looking beast available."

"We won't find one now."

"Why not?"

"Because bookings are done months in advance."

"We don't have months. We have days." Nina leaned her aching head against the cushions.

"Are you there? Nina?"

Nina opened her eyes and pulled her robe tighter. "Let me call my aunt."

"That's a risk. What if she decides you can't manage this show?"

Mom's heels clacked down the hall. She blew Nina a kiss and grabbed her purse on her way out the door. Her eyes were too bright. The sway of her hips and tilt to her chin could only mean one thing.

Nina hit the mute button on her phone. "Mom?"

"Yes?"

"It's a man, isn't it?"

"What are you talking about?"

"Your lunch date." Nina steeled herself for confirmation.

Mom fluttered her fingers in a goodbye wave and shut the door.

The last thing Mom needed was another man. Ironically it was the one thing Nina *did* need. She unmuted her phone. "I'll call you back, Karoline."

The Pacific Northwest Fashion Blogger of the Year award meant even more now.

Made in United States
Orlando, FL
02 September 2024